The Rising of the Court by Henry Lawson

Henry Archibald Hertzberg Lawson was born on the 17th June 1867 in a town on the Grenfell goldfields of New South Wales, Australia.

As a youth an ear infection had left him partially deaf and by fourteen he had lost his hearing completely.

He immersed himself in books to make up for the difficulties of a classroom education but later failed to gain entry to a University.

His first published poem was 'A Song of the Republic' in The Bulletin on 1st October 1887. This was quickly followed by other poems with one recognising him as "a youth whose poetic genius here speaks eloquently for itself."

In 1892, The Bulletin engaged him for an inland trip where he could write articles about the harsh realities of life in drought-stricken New South Wales. This resulted in his contributions to the Bulletin Debate and became the experience for a number of his stories in subsequent years. For Lawson this was an eye-opening period. His grim view of the outback was far removed from the romantic idyll of contemporary poetry and literature.

In 1896, Lawson married Bertha Bredt, Jr. but the marriage ended in June 1903. They had two children.

Despite this Lawson was finding his way in the literary world and achieving recognition. His most successful prose collection 'While the Billy Boils', was published in 1896. In it he virtually reinvented Australian realism.

His writing style of short, sharp sentences with honed and sparse descriptions created a personal writing style that defined Australians: dryly laconic, passionately egalitarian and deeply humane.

Sadly, for Lawson despite his growing recognition and fame he became withdrawn and unable to take part in the usual routines of life. His struggles with alcohol and mental health issues continued to drain him. His once prolific literary output began to decline. At times he was destitute mainly due, despite good sales and an enthusiastic audience, to ruinous publishing deals he had entered into.

Henry Archibald Hertzberg Lawson died, of cerebral hemorrhage, in Abbotsford, Sydney on 2nd September 1922.

Index of Contents

THE EXCISEMAN
MATESHIP IN SHAKESPEARE'S ROME
HENRY LAWSON – A SHORT BIOGRAPHY
HENRY LAWSON – A CONCISE BIBLIOGRAPHY

THE RISING OF THE COURT

Oh, then tell us, Sings and Judges, where our meeting is to be, when the laws of men are nothing, and our spirits all are free when the laws of men are nothing, and no wealth can hold the fort, There'll be thirst for mighty brewers at the Rising of the Court.

The same dingy court room, deep and dim, like a well, with the clock high up on the wall, and the doors low down in it; with the bench, which, with some gilding, might be likened to a gingerbread imitation of a throne; the royal arms above it and the little witness box to one side, where so many honest poor people are bullied, insulted and laughed at by third-rate blackguardly little "lawyers," and so many pitiful, pathetic and noble lies are told by pitiful sinners and disreputable heroes for a little liberty for a lost self, or for the sake of a friend—of a "pal" or a "cobber." The same overworked and underpaid magistrate trying to keep his attention fixed on the same old miserable scene before him; as a weary, overworked and underpaid journalist or author strives to keep his attention fixed on his proofs. The same row of big, strong, healthy, good-natured policemen trying not to grin at times; and the police-court solicitors ("the place stinks with 'em," a sergeant told me) wrangling over some miserable case for a crust, and the "reporters," shabby some of them, eager to get a brutal joke for their papers out of the accumulated mass of misery before them, whether it be at the expense of the deaf, blind, or crippled man, or the alien.

And opposite the bench, the dock, divided by a partition, with the women to the left and the men to the right, as it is on the stairs or the block in polite society. They bring children here no longer. The same shaking, wild-eyed, blood-shot-eyed and blear-eyed drunks and disorderlies, though some of the women have nerves yet; and the same decently dressed, but trembling and conscience-stricken little wretch up for petty larceny or something, whose motor car bosses of a big firm have sent a solicitor, "manager," or some understrapper here to prosecute and give evidence.

But, over there, on a form to one side of the bench-opposite the witness box—and as the one bright spot in this dark, and shameful, and useless scene—and in a patch of sunlight from the skylight as it happens—sit representatives of the Prisoners' Aid Society, Prison Gate and Rescue Brigades, etc. (one or two of the ladies in nurses' uniforms), who are come to help us and to fight for us against the Law of their Land and of ours, God help us!

Mrs Johnson, of Red Rock Lane, is here, and her rival in revolution, One-Eyed Kate, and Cock-Eyed Sal, and one or two of the other aristocrats of the alley. And the weeping bedraggled remains of what was once, and not so long ago, a pretty, slight, fair-haired and blue-eyed Australian girl. She is up for inciting One-Eyed Kate to resist the police. Also, Three-Pea Ginger, Stousher, and Wingy, for some participation in the row amongst the aforementioned ladies. (Wingy, by the way, is a ratty little one-armed man, whose case is usually described in the head-line, as "A 'Armless Case," by one of our great dailies.) And their pals are waiting outside in the vestibule—Frowsy Kate (The Red Streak), Boko Bill, Pincher and his "piece," etc., getting together the stuff for the possible fines, and the ten-bob fee for the lawyer, in one case, and ready to swear to anything, if called upon. And I myself—though I have not yet entered Red Rock Lane Society—on bail, on a charge of "plain drunk." It was "drunk and disorderly" by the way, but a kindly sergeant changed it to plain drunk (though I always thought my drunk was ornamental).

Yet I am not ashamed—only comfortably dulled and a little tired—dully interested and observant, and hopeful for the sunlight presently. We low persons get too great a contempt for things to feel much ashamed at any time; and this very contempt keeps many of us from "reforming." We hear too many lies sworn that we know to be lies, and see too many unjust and brutal things done that we know to be brutal and unjust.

But let us go back a bit, and suppose we are still waiting for the magistrate, and think of Last Night. "Silence!"—but from no human voice this time. The whispering, shuffling, and clicking of the court typewriter ceases, the scene darkens, and the court is blotted out as a scene is blotted out from the sight of a man who has thrown himself into a mesmeric trance. And:

Drink—lurid recollection of being "searched"—clang of iron cell door, and I grope for and crawl on to the slanting plank. Period of oblivion—or the soul is away in some other world. Clang of cell door again, and soul returns in a hurry to take heed of another soul, belonging to a belated drunk on the plank by my side. Other soul says:

"Gotta match?"

So we're not in hell yet.

We fumble and light up. They leave us our pipes, tobacco and matches; presently, one knocks with his pipe on the iron trap of the door and asks for water, which is brought in a tin pint-pot. Then follow intervals of smoking, incoherent mutterings that pass for conversation, borrowings of matches, knockings with the pannikin on the cell door wicket or trap for more water, matches, and bail; false and fitful starts into slumber perhaps—or wild attempts at flight on the part of our souls into that other world that the sober and sane know nothing of; and, gradually, suddenly it seems, reason (if this world is reasonable) comes back.

"What's your trouble!"

"Don't know. Bomb outrage, perhaps."

"Drunk?"

"Yes."

"What's yours!"

"Same boat."

But presently he is plainly uneasy (and I am getting that way, too, to tell the truth), and, after moving about, and walking up and down in the narrow space as well as we can, he "rings up" another policeman, who happens to be the fat one who is to be in charge all night.

"Wot's up here?"

"What have I been up to?"

"Killin' a Chinaman. Go to sleep."

Policeman peers in at me inquiringly, but I forbear to ask questions.

Blankets are thrown in by a friend of mine in the force, though we are not entitled to them until we are bailed or removed to the "paddock" (the big drunks' dormitory and dining cell at the Central), and we proceed to make ourselves comfortable. My mate wonders whether he asked them to send to his wife to get bail, and hopes he didn't.

They have left our wicket open, seeing, or rather hearing, that we are quiet. But they have seemingly left some other wickets open also, for from a neighbouring cell comes the voice of Mrs Johnson holding forth. The locomotive has apparently just been run into the cleaning sheds, and her fires have not had time to cool. They say that Mrs Johnson was a "lady once," like many of her kind; that she is not a "bad woman"—that is, not a woman of loose character—but gets money sent to her from somewhere—from her "family," or her husband, perhaps. But when she lets herself loose—or, rather, when the beer lets her loose—she is a tornado and a terror in Red Rock Lane, and it is only her fierce, practical kindness to her unfortunate or poverty-stricken sisters in her sober moments that keeps her forgiven in that classic thoroughfare. She can certainly speak "like a lady" when she likes, and like an intelligent, even a clever, woman—not like a "woman of the world," but as a woman who knew and knows the world, and is in hell. But now her language is the language of a rough shearer in a "rough shed" on a blazing hot day.

After a while my mate calls out to her:

"Oh! for God's sake give it a rest!"

Whereupon Mrs Johnson straightway opens on him and his ancestry, and his mental, moral, and physical condition—especially the latter. She accuses him of every crime known to Christian countries and some Asiatic and ancient ones. She wants to know how long he has been out of jail for kicking his wife to pieces that time when she was up as a witness against him, and whether he is in for the same thing again? (She has never set eyes on him, by the way, nor he on her.)

He calls back that she is not a respectable woman, and he knows all about her.

Thereupon she shrieks at him and bangs and kicks at her door, and demands his name and address. It would appear that she is a respectable woman, and hundreds can prove it, and she is going to make him prove it in open court.

He calls back that his name is Percy Reginald Grainger, and his town residence is "The Mansions," Macleay Street, next to Mr Isaacs, the magistrate, and he also gives her the address of his solicitor.

She bangs and shrieks again, and states that she will get his name from the charge sheet in the morning and have him up for criminal libel, and have his cell mate up as a witness—and hers, too. But just here a policeman comes along and closes her wicket with a bang and cuts her off, so that her statements become indistinct, or come only as shrieks from a lost soul in an underground dungeon. He also threatens to cut us off and smother us if we don't shut up. I wonder whether they've got her in the padded cell.

We settle down again, but presently my fellow captive nudges me and says: "Listen!" From another cell comes the voice of a woman singing—the girl who is in for "inciting to resist, your worship," in fact. "Listen!" he says, "that woman could sing once." Her voice is low and sweet and plaintive, as of a woman who had been a singer but had lost her voice. And what do you think it is?

The crowd in accents hushed reply—"Jesus of Nazareth passeth by."

Mrs Johnson's cell is suddenly silent. Then, not mimickingly, mockingly, or scornfully, but as if the girl is a champion of Jesus of Nazareth, and is hurt at the ignorance of the multitude, and pities Him:

Now who is this Jesus of Nazareth, say?

The policeman, coming along the passage, closes the wicket in her door, but softly this time, and not before we catch the plaintive words again.

The crowd in accents hushed reply "Jesus of Nazareth passeth by."

My fellow felon throws the blanket off him impatiently, sits up with a jerk, and gropes for his pipe.

"God!" he says. "But this is red hot! Have you got another match?"

I wonder what the Nazarene would have to say about it.

Sleep for a while. I wonder whether they'll give us time, or we'll be able to sleep some of our sins off in the end, as we sleep our drink off here? Then "The Paddock" and day light; but there's little time for the Paddock here, for we must soon be back in court. The men borrow and lend and divide tobacco, lend even pipes, while some break up hard tobacco and roll cigarettes with bits of newspaper. If it is Sunday morning, even those who have no hope for bail, and have long horrible day and night before them, will sometimes join in a cheer as the more fortunate are bailed. But the others have tea and bread and butter brought to them by one of the Prisoners' Aid Societies, who ask for no religion in return. They come to save bodies, and not to fish for souls. The men walk up and down and to and fro, and cross and recross incessantly, as caged men and animals always do—and as some uncaged men do too.

"Any of you gentlemen want breakfast?" Those who have money and appetites order; some order for the sake of the tea alone; and some "shout" two or three extra breakfasts for those who had nothing on them when they were run in. We low people can be very kind to each other in trouble. But now it's time to call us out by the lists, marshal us up in the passage and draft us into court. Ladies first. But I forgot that I am out on bail, and that the foregoing belongs to another occasion. Or was it only imagination, or hearsay? Journalists have got themselves run in before now, in order to see and hear and feel and smell for themselves—and write.

"Silence! Order in the Court." I come like a shot out of my nightmare, or trance, or what you will, and we all rise as the magistrate takes his seat. None of us noticed him come in, but he's there, and I've a quaint idea that he bowed to his audience. Kindly, humorous Mr Isaacs, whom we have lost, always gave me that idea. And, while he looks over his papers, the women seem to group themselves, unconsciously as it were, with Mrs Johnson as front centre, as though they depended on her in some vague way. She has slept it off and tidied, or been tidied, up, and is as clear-headed as she ever will be. Crouching directly behind her, supported and comforted on one side by One-Eyed Kate, and on the other by Cock-Eyed Sal, is the poor bedraggled little resister of the Law, sobbing convulsively, her breasts and thin shoulders heaving and shaking under her openwork blouse—the girl who seemed to pity Jesus of Nazareth last night in her cell. There's very little inciting to resist about her now. Most women can cry when they like, I know, and many have cried men to jail and the gallows; but here in this place, if a woman's tears can avail her anything, who, save perhaps a police-court solicitor and gentleman-by-Act-of-Parliament, would, or dare, raise a sneer.

I wonder what the Nazarene would have to say about it if He came in to speak for her. But probably they'd send Him to the receiving house as a person of unsound mind, or give Him worse punishment for drunkenness and contempt of court.

His Worship looks up.

Mrs Johnson (from the dock): "Good morning, Mr Isaacs. How do you do? You're looking very well this morning, Mr Isaacs."

His Worship (from the Bench): "Thank you, Mrs Johnson. I'm feeling very well this, morning."

There's a pause, but there is no "laughter." The would-be satellites don't know whom the laugh might be against. His Worship bends over the papers again, and I can see that he is having trouble with that quaintly humorous and kindly smile, or grin, of his. He has as hard a job to control his smile and get it off his face as some magistrates have to get a smile on to theirs. And there's a case coming by and by that he'll have to look a bit serious over. However—

"Jane Johnson!"

Mrs Johnson is here present, and reminds the Sergeant that she is.

Then begins, or does begin in most courts, the same dreary old drone, like the giving out of a hymn, of the same dreary old charge:

"You—Are—Charged—With—Being—Drunk—And—Disorderly—In—Such—And— Such—A—Street— How—Do—You—Plead—Guilty—Or—Not—Guilty?" But they are less orthodox here. The "disorderly" has dropped out of Mrs Johnson's charge somehow, on the way from the charge room. I don't know what has been going on behind the scenes, but, anyway, it is Christmas- time, and the Sergeant seems anxious to let Mrs Johnson off lightly. It means anything from twenty-four hours or five shillings to three months on the Island for her. The lawyers and the police—especially the lawyers—are secretly afraid of Mrs Johnson.

However, again—

The Sergeant: "This woman has not been here for six weeks, your Worship."

Mrs Johnson (who has him set and has been waiting for him for a year or so): "It's a damned lie, Mr Isaacs. I was here last Wednesday!" Then, after a horrified pause in the Court: "But I beg your pardon, Mr Isaacs."

His Worship's head goes down again. The "laughter" doesn't come here, either. There is a whispered consultation, and (it being Christmas-time) they compromise with Mrs Johnson for "five shillings or the risin'," and she thanks his Worship and is escorted out, rather more hurriedly than is comportable with her dignity, for she remarks about it.

The members of the Johnsonian sisterhood have reason to be thankful for the "lift" she has given them, for they all get off lightly, and even the awful resister of Law-an'-order is forgiven. Mrs Johnson has money and is waiting outside to stand beers for them; she always shouts for the boys when she has it. And—what good does it all do?

It is very hard to touch the heart of a woman who is down, though they are intensely sympathetic amongst themselves. It is nearly as hard as it is to combat the pride of a hard-working woman in poverty. It was such women as Mrs Johnson, One-Eyed Kate, and their sisters who led Paris to Versailles; and a King and a Queen died for it. It is such women as Mrs Johnson and One-Eyed Kate and their sisters who will lead a greater Paris to a greater Versailles some day, and many "Trust" kings and queens, and their princes and princesses shall die for it. And that reminds me of two reports in a recent great daily:

Miss Angelina De Tapps, the youngest daughter of the well-known great family of brewers, was united in the holy bonds of matrimony to Mr Reginald Wells—(here follows a long account of the smart society wedding). The happy pair leave en route for Europe per the —next Friday.

Jane Johnson, an old offender, again faced the music before Mr Isaacs, S.M., at the Central yesterday morning—(here follows a "humorous" report of the case).

Next time poor Mrs Johnson will leave en route for "Th' Island" and stay there three months.

The sisters join Mrs Johnson, who has some money and takes them to a favourite haunt and shouts for them—as she does for the boys sometimes. Their opinions on civilization are not to be printed.

Ginger and Wingy get off with the option, and, though the fine is heavy, it is paid. They adjourn with Boko Bill, and their politics are lurid.

Squinny Peters (plain drunk—five bob or the risin'), who is peculiar for always paying his fine, elects to take it out this time. It appears that the last time Squinny got five bob or the risin' he ante'd up the splosh like a man, and the court rose immediately, to Squinny's intense disgust. He isn't taking any chances this time.

Wild-Flowers-Charley, who recently did a fortnight, and has been out on bail, has had a few this morning, and, in spite of warnings from and promises to friends, insists on making a statement, though by simply pleading guilty he might get off easily. The statement lasts some ten minutes. Mr Isaacs listens patiently and politely and remarks:

"Fourteen days."

Charley saw the humour of it afterwards, he says.

But what good does it all do?

I had no wish to treat drunkenness frivolously in beginning this sketch; I have seen women in the horrors—that ought to be enough.

"ROLL UP AT TALBRAGAR"

Jack Denver died at Talbragar when Christmas Eve began,
And there was sorrow round the place, for Denver was a man;
Jack Denver's wife bowed down her head—her daughter's grief was wild,
And big Ben Duggan by the bed stood sobbing like a child.
 But big Ben Duggan saddled up, and galloped fast and far,
To raise the longest funeral ever seen on Talbragar.

Ben Duggan.

Both funerals belonged to Big Ben Duggan in a way, though Jack Denver was indirectly the cause of both.

Jack Denver was reckoned the most popular man in the district (outside the principal township)—a white man and a straight man—a white boss and a straight sportsman. He was a squatter, though a small one; a real squatter who lived on his run and worked with his men—no dummy, super, manager for a bank, or swollen cockatoo about Jack Denver. He was on the committees at agricultural shows and sports, great at picnics and dances, beloved by school children at school feasts (I wonder if they call them feasts still), giver of extra or special prizes, mostly sovs. and half-sovs., for foot races, etc.; leading spirit for the scrub district in electioneering campaigns—they went as right as men could go in the politics of those days who watched and went the way Jack Denver went; header of subscription lists for burnt-out, flooded-out, sick, hurt, dead or killed or otherwise knocked-out selectors and others, or their families; barracker and agitator for new provisional schools, assister of his Reverence and little bush chapels, friend of all manner of wanderers—careless, good-hearted scamps in trouble, broken-hearted new chums, wrecks and failures and outcasts of any colour or creed, and especially of old King Jimmy and the swiftly vanishing remnant of his tribe. His big slab-and-shingle and brick-floored kitchen, with its skillions, built on more generous plans and specifications than even the house itself, was the wanderer's goal and home in bad weather. And—yes, owner, on a small scale, of racehorses, and a keen sportsman.

Jack Denver and Big Ben Duggan were boys together on the old selections, and at the new provisional bark school at Pipeclay; they went into the Great North-West together "where all the rovers go"—stock-riding and droving and overlanding, and came back after a few years bronzed and seasoned and with wild yarns.

Jack married and settled down on a small run his father had bought near Talbragar, and his generous family of tall, straight bush boys and tall, straight bush girls grew up and had their sweethearts. But, when Jack married, Big Ben Duggan went back again, up into Queensland and the Great North-West, with a makeshift mate who had also lost his mate through marriage. Ever and again, after one, and two, and three years—the periods of absence lengthening as the years went on—Big Ben Duggan would come back home, and stay a while (till the Great North-West began to call insistently) at Denver's, where he would be welcomed jubilantly by all—even the baby who had never seen him—for there was "something about the man." And, until late on the night of his return, he and Jack would sit by the fire in winter, or outside on the woodheap in summer, and yarn long and fondly about the Wide Places, and strange things they knew and understood.

How sudden things are! Ben was back (just in time for the holidays and the Mudgee races) out of the level lands, where distance dwells in her halls of shimmering haze, after following her for five years.

They were riding home from the races, the women and children in carts and buggies, the men and boys on horseback—of course. They raced each other along the road, across short cuts, through scrub and timber, and back to the slow-coming overloaded vehicles again, some riding wildly and recklessly. Jack Denver was amongst them, his heart warmed with good luck at the races, good whisky to wet it, and the return of his old mate. "We're as good as the best of the young 'uns yet, Ben!" he cried, as they swung through the trees. "Ain't we, you old—?"

And then and there it happened.

A new chum suggested that Jack had more than he thought aboard and was thrown from his horse; but the new chum was repudiated with scorn and bad words and indignation by bushmen and bushwomen alike—as indeed he would be by any bushman who had seen a drunken rider ride.

"I learnt him to ride when he was a kiddy about so high," said old Break-the-News Fosbery, resentfully gasping and gulping, "and Jack wasn't thrown." It was thought at first that his horse had shied and run him against a tree, or under an overhanging branch; but Ben Duggan had seen it, and explained the thing to the doctor with that strange calmness or quietness that comes to men in the midst of a life's grief. Jack was riding loosely, and swung forward just as the filly, a fresh young thing, threw back her head; and it struck him with sledge-hammer force, full in the face.

He was dead, even before they got him to Anderson's Halfway Inn. There was wild racing back to town for doctors, and some accidents; one horse was killed and another ridden to death. Others went as a forlorn hope in search of Doc. Wild, eccentric Yankee bush "quack," who had once saved one of Denver's little girls from diphtheria; others, again, for Peter M'Laughlan, bush missionary, to face the women—for they couldn't.

Big Ben Duggan, blubbering unashamed by the bedside, put his hand on Mrs Denver's shoulder, as she crouched there, wild-eyed, like a hunted thing. "Nev—never mind, Mrs Denver!" he blurted out, with a note as of indignation and defiance—just for all the world as if Jack Denver had done a wrong thing and the district was down on him—"he'll have the longest funeral ever seen in these parts! Leave that to me." Then some of the women took her out to her daughter's. Big Ben Duggan gave terse instructions to some of the young riders about, and then, taking the best and freshest horse, the cross-country scrub swallowed him—west. The young men jumped on their horses and rode, fan-like, east.

They took Jack Denver home. They always took their dead home first, whenever possible, and no matter the distance, before taking them to their last long home; and they do it yet, I suppose. They are not always so particular about it in cities, from what I've seen.

But this was a strange funeral. They had arranged mattress and sheet in the bottom of a four-wheeler, and covered him with sheet, blanket, and quilt, though the weather was warm; and over the body, from side to side of the trap, they had stretched the big dark-green table-cloth from Anderson's dining-room. The long, ghostly, white, cleared government road between the dark walls of timber in the moonlight. The buggies and carts behind, and the dead-white faces and glistening or despairingly staring eyes of the women—wife, daughters, and nieces, and those who had come to help and comfort. The men—sons and brothers, and few mates and chums and sweethearts—riding to right and left like a bodyguard, to comfort and be comforted who needed comfort.

Now and again a brother or son—mostly a brother—riding close to the wheel, would suddenly throw out his arm on the mud splasher, of buggy or cart, and, laying his head on it, sob as he rode, careless of tyre and spokes, till a woman pushed him off gently:

"Take care of the wheel, Jim—mind the wheel."

The eldest son held the most painful position, by his mother's side in the first buggy, supported by an aunt on the other side, while somebody led his horse. In the next buggy, between two daughters, sat a young fellow who was engaged to one of them—they were to be married after the holidays. The poor girls were white and worn out; he had an arm round each, and now and again they rested their heads on his shoulders. The younger girl would sleep by fits and starts, the sleep of exhaustion, and start up half laughing and happy, to be stricken wild-eyed the next moment by terrible reality. Some couldn't realize it at all—and to most of them all things were very dreamy, unreal and far away on that lonely, silent road in the moonlight—silent save for the slow, stumbling hoofs of tired horses, and the deliberate, half-hesitating clack-clack of wheel-boxes on the axles.

Ben Duggan rode hard, as grief-stricken men ride—and walk. At Cooyal he woke up the solitary storekeeper and told him the news; then along that little-used old road for some miles both ways, and back again, rousing prospectors and fossickers, the butcher of the neighbourhood, clearers, fencers, and timber-getters, in hut and tent.

"Who's that?"

"What's up?"

"What's the matter?"

"Ben Duggan! Jack Denver's dead! Killed ridin' home from the races! Funeral's to-morrow. Roll up at Talbragar or the nearest point you can get to on the government road. Tell the neighbours and folks."

"Good God! How did it happen?"

But the hoofs of Ben's horse would be clattering or thudding away into the distance.

He struck through to Dunne's selection—his brother-in-law, who had not been to the races; then to Ross's farm—Old Ross was against racing, but struck a match at once and said something to his auld wife about them black trousers that belonged to the black coat and vest.

Then Ben swung to the left and round behind the spurs to the school at Old Pipeclay, where he told the schoolmaster. Then west again to Morris's and Schneider's lonely farms in the deep estuary of Long Gully, and through the gully to the Mudgee-Gulgong road at New Pipeclay. The long, dark, sullenly-brooding gully through which he had gone to school in the glorious bush sunshine with Jack Denver, and his sweetheart—now but three hours his hopelessly-stricken widow; Bertha Lambert, Ben's sweetheart—married now, and newly a grandmother; Harry Dale—drowned in the Lachlan; Lucy Brown—Harry's school-day and boy-and-girl sweetheart—dead; and—and all the rest of them. Far away, far away—and near away: up in Queensland and out on the wastes of the Never-Never. Riding and camping, hardship and comfort, monotony and adventure, drought, flood, blacks, and fire; sprees and—the rest of it. Long dry stretches on Dead Man's Track. Cutting across the country in No Man's Land where there were no tracks into the Unknown. Chancing it and damning it. Ill luck and good luck. Laughing at it afterwards and joking at it always; he and Jack—always he and Jack—till Jack got married. The children used to say Long Gully was haunted, and always hurried through it after sunset. It was haunted enough now all right.

But, raising the gap at the head of the gully, he woke suddenly and came back from the hazy, lazy plains; the

Level lands where Distance hides in her halls of shimmering haze, And where her toiling dreamers ride towards her all their days;

where "these things" are ever far away, and Distance ever near—and whither he had drifted, the last hour, with Jack Denver, from the old Slab School.

"I wonder whether old Fosbery's got through yet?" he muttered, with nervous anxiety, as he looked down on the cluster of farms and scattered fringe of selections in the broad moonlight. "I wonder if he's got there yet?" Then, as if to reassure himself: "He must have started an hour before me, and the old man can ride yet." He rode down towards a farm on Pipeclay Creek, about the centre of the cluster of farms, vineyards, and orchards.

Old Fosbery—otherwise Break-the-News—was a character round there. If he was handy and no woman to be had, he was always sent to break the news to the wife of a digger or bushman who had met with an accident. He was old, and world-wise, and had great tact—also great experience in such matters. Bad news had been broken to him so many times that he had become hardened to it, and he had broken bad news so often that he had come to take a decided sort of pleasure in it—just as some bushman are great at funerals and will often travel miles to advise, and organize, and comfort, and potter round a burying and are welcomed. They had broken the news to old Fosbery when his boy went wrong and was "taken" ("when they took Jim"). They had broken the news to old Fosbery when his daughter, Rose, went wrong, and bolted with Flash Jack Redmond. They had broken the news to the old man when young Ted was thrown from his horse and killed. They had broken the news to the old man when the unexpected child of his old age and hopes was accidentally burnt to death. So the old man knew how it felt.

The farm was the home of one of Jack Denver's married sisters, and, as there was no woman to go so far in the night they had sent old Fosbery to tell her. Folks were most uneasy and anxious, by the way, when they saw old Fosbery coming unexpectedly, and sometimes some of them got a bad start—but it helped break the news.

"Well, if he ain't there, I suppose I'll have to do it," thought Ben as he passed quietly through the upper sliprails and neared the house. "The old man might have knocked up or got drunk after all. Anyway, no one might come in the morning till it's too late—it always happens that way—and—besides, the women'll want time to look up their black things."

But, turning the corner of the cow-yard, he gave a sigh of relief as he saw old Fosbery's horse tied up. They were up, and the big kitchen lighted; he caught a glimpse of a shock of white hair and bushy white eyebrows that could have belonged to no one except old Break-the-News. They were sitting at the table, the tearful wife pouring out tea, and by the tokens Ben knew that old Fosbery had been very successful. He rode quietly to the lower sliprails, let them down softly, led his horse carefully over them, put them up cautiously, and stood in a main road again. He paused to think, leaning one arm on his saddle and tickling the nape of his neck with his little finger; his jaw dropped, reflecting and grief forgotten in the business on hand, and the horse "gave" to him, thinking he was about to mount. He was tired—weary with that strange energetic weariness that cannot rest. It was five miles from Mudgee and the news was known there and must have spread a bit already; but the bulk of the Gulgong and Gulgong Road race-goers had passed here before the accident. Anyway, he thought he might as well go over and tell old Buckolts, of the big vineyard, across the creek, who was a great admirer of Jack Denver and had been drinking with him at the races that day. Old Buckolts was a man of weight in the district, and was always referred to by all from his old wife down, as "der boss," and by no other term. The old slab farmhouse and skillions and out-houses, and the new square brick house built in front, were all asleep in the moonlight. The dogs woke the old man first (as was generally the case), as Ben opened the big white home gate and passed through without dismounting.

"Who's dat? Who voss die [there]?" shouted the old man as the horse's hoofs crunched on the white creek-bed gravel between the two houses.

"Ben Duggan!"

"Vot voss der matter?"

"Jack Denver's dead—killed riding home from the races."

"Vot dat you say?"

Ben repeated.

"Go avay! Go home and go to sleep! You voss shoking—and trunk. Vat for you gum by my house mit a seely cock mit der bull shtory at dis hour of der night?"

"It's only too true, Mr Buckolts," said Ben. "I wish to God it wasn't."

"You've got der yoomps, Pen. Go to der poomp and poomp on your head and den turn in someveers till ter morning. I tells von of der pot's to gif you a nip and show you a poonk. Vy! I trink mit Shack Denver not twelf hour ago!"

But Ben persisted: "I'm not drunk, Mr Buckolts, and I ain't got the horrors—I wish to God I was an' had. Poor Jack was killed near Anderson's, riding home, about six o'clock."

Though Ben couldn't see him, he could feel and hear by his tones, that old Buckolts sat up in bed suddenly.

"Mein Gott! How did it happen, Pen?"

Ben told him.

"Ven and veer voss der funeral?"

Ben told him.

"Frett! Shonny! Villie! Sharley!" shouted the old man at the top of his voice to the boys sleeping in the old house. "Get up and pring all der light horses in from der patticks, and gif dem a goot feet mit plenty corn; and get der double-parreled puggy ant der sinkle puggy and der three spring carts retty. Dere vill pe peoples vanting lifts to-morrow. Ant get der harnesses and sattles retty. Vake up, olt vomans!" (Mrs Buckolts must have been awake by this time.) "Call der girls ant see to dere plack tresses. Py Gott, ve moost do dis thing in style. Does his poor sister know over dere across the creeks, Pen? Durn out! you lazy, goot-for-noddings, or I will chain you up on an ants' bed mit a rope like a tog; do you not hear that Shack Denver voss dett?"

"I vill sent some of der girls over dere first thing in der morning. Holt on, Pen, ant I vill sent you out some vine."

Ben rode with the news to Lee's farm where Maurice Lee—at feud with Buckolts and a silent man—was, for he had known Denver all his life, and had gone, in his young days, on a long droving trip with him and Ben Duggan.

A little later Ben returned to the main road on a fresh horse. He turned towards Gulgong, and rode hard; past the new bark provisional school and along the sidings. He left the news at Con O'Donnell's lonely tin grocery and sly-grog shop, perched on the hillside—("God forgive us all!" said Con O'Donnell). He left the news at the tumble-down public-house, among the huts and thistles and goats that were left of the Log Paddock Rush. There were goats on the veranda and the place seemed dead; but there were startled replies and inquiries and matches struck. He left the news at Newton's selection, and Old Bones Farm, and at Foley's at the foot of Lowe's Peak, close under the gap between Peak and Granite Ridge. Then he turned west, at right angles to the main road, and took a track that was deserted except for one farm and on every alternate Sunday. He passed the lonely little slab bush "chapel" of the locality, that broke startlingly out of the scrub by the track side as he reached it; and left the news at Southwick's farm at the end of the blind track. At more than one farm he left the bushwoman hurriedly looking up her "black things;" and at more than one, one of the boys getting his bridle to catch his horse and ride elsewhere with the news.

Ben rode back, through the moonlight and the moon-shadow haunted paddocks, and the naked, white, ringbarked trees, along Snakes Creek, parallel with the main road he had recently travelled till he struck Pipeclay Creek again lower down. He turned down the track towards the river, and at the junction left word at Lowe's—one of the old land-grant families. The dogs woke an old handy man (who had been "sent out" in past ages for "knocking a donkey off a hen-roost"—as most of them were) and Ben told him to tell the family.

At Belinfante's Bridge across the Cudgegong Ben struck a big camp of bullock-drivers, some going down with wool and some going back for more.

"Hold on, Ben," cried Jimmy Nowlett, from his hammock under his wagon as Ben was riding off—"Hold on a minute! I want to look at yer."

Jimmy got his head out of his bunk very cautiously and carefully, and his body after it—there were nut ends of bolts, a heavy axle, and extremely hard projections, points, and corners within a very few short inches of his chaff-filled sugar-bag pillow. Slipping cannily on to his hands and knees, he crawled out under the tail-board, dragging his "moles" after him, and stood outside in the moonlight shaking himself into his trousers.

Jimmy was a little man who always wore a large size in moleskins—for some reason best known to himself—or more probably for no reason at all; or because of a habit he'd got into accidentally years ago—or because of the motherly trousers his mother used to build for him when he was a boy. And he always shook himself into his pants after the manner of a woman shaking a pillow into a clean slip; his chin down on his chest and his jaw dropped, as if he'd take himself in his teeth, after the manner of the woman with a pillow, were he not prevented by sound anatomical reasons.

"You look reg'lerly tuckered out, Ben," he said, "an' yer horse could do with a spell too. Git down, man, and have a pint er tea and a bite."

Ben got down wearily and knew at once how knocked up he was. He sat right down on the hard ground, embracing and drawing up his knees, and felt as if he'd like never to get up again: while Jimmy shook some chaff and corn that he carried for his riding hack into a box for the horse, and his travelling mate, Billy Grimshaw, lifted his big namesake half full of cold tea, on to the glowing coals by the burning log—looking just like an orang-outang in a Crimean shirt.

Ben got a fresh horse at Alfred Gentle's farm under the shadow of Granite Ridge, and then on to Canadian (th' Canadian Lead of the roaring days), which had been saved from the usual fate by becoming a farming township. Here he roused and told the storekeeper. Then up the creek to Home Rule, dreariest of deserted diggings.

He struck across the ages-haunted bush, and up Chinaman's Creek, past "the Chinamen's Graves," and through the scrub and over the ridges for the Talbragar Road. For he had to see Jack Denver home from start to finish.

Glaring, hot and dusty, lay the long, white road; coated with dust that felt greasy to the touch and taste. The coffin was in a four-wheeled trap, for the solitary hearse that Mudgee boasted then was to meet them some three miles out of town—at the racecourse, as it happened, by one of those eternal ironies of fate. (Jones, the undertaker, had had another job that morning.) The long string of buggies and carts and horsemen; other buggies and carts and horsemen drawn respectfully back amongst the trees here and there along the route; male hats off and held rigidly vertical with right ears as the coffin passed; and drivers waiting for a chance to draw into the line.

Think of it; up early on the first morning, a long day at the races, a long journey home, awake and up all night with grief and sympathy. Some of the men had ridden till daylight; the women, worn out and exhausted, had perhaps an hour or so of sleep towards morning—yet they were all there, except Ben

Duggan, on the long, hot, dusty road back, heads swimming in the heat and faces and hands coated with perspiration and dust—and never, never once breaking out of a slow walk. It would have been the same had it been pouring with rain. I have seen funerals trotting fast in London, and they are trotting more and more in Australian cities, with only "the time" for an excuse. But in the bush I have never seen a funeral faster than the slowest of walks no matter who or what might wait, or what might happen or be lost. They stood by their dead well out there. Maybe some of the big, simple souls had a sort of vague idea that the departed would stand a better show if accompanied as far as possible by the greatest possible number of friends—"barrackers," so to speak.

Here all the shallow and involuntary sham of it, the shirking of a dull and irksome duty—a bore, though the route be only a mile or so. The satisfied undertaker, and the hard-up professional mutes and mourners in seedy, mouldy, greeny-black, and with boozers' faces and noses and a constant craving for beer to help them bear up against their grief and keep their mock solemn faces. Out there you were carried to the hearse or trap from your home, and from the hearse or trap to your grave—and with infinite carefulness and gentleness—on the shoulders of men, and of men who had known and loved you.

There had been wonder and waiting in the morning for Ben Duggan; and the women especially, on the way home, when free from restraint, were greatly indignant against him. To think that he should break out and go on the drunk on this day of all days, when his oldest mate and friend was being carried to his grave. The men, knowing how he had ridden all night, found great excuses; but later on some grew anxious and wondered what could have become of him.

Some, returning home by a short cut, passed over Dead Man's Gap beyond Lowe's Peak.

"Wonder what could have become of Ben Duggan." mused one, as they rode down.

There and then their wonders ceased.

A party of road-clearers had been at work along the bottom, and there was much smoke from the burning-off, which must have made the track dim and vague and uncertain at night. Just at the foot of the gap, clear of the rough going, a newly-fallen tree lay across the track. It was stripped—had been stripped late the previous afternoon, in fact; and, well, you won't know, what a log like that is when the sap is well up until you have stepped casually on to it to take a look round. A confident skip, with your boot soles well greased, on to the ice in a glaciarium for the first time would be nothing to it in its results, I fancy. (I remember we children used to scrape the sap off, and eat it with satisfaction, if not with relish—white box I think the trees were.)

Ben must have broken into a canter as he reached the level, as indeed his horse's tracks showed he did, and the horse must have blundered in the smoke, or jumped too long or too short; anyway, his long slithering shoe marks were in the sap on the log, and he lay there with a broken leg and shoulder. He had struck it near the stump and the sharp edge of an outcrop of rock.

There was more breakneck riding, and they got a cart and some bedding and carried Ben to Anderson's, which was handiest, if not nearest, and there was more wild and reckless riding for the doctor.

One got a gun, and rode back to shoot the horse.

Ben's case was hopeless from the first. He was hurt close to that big heart of his, as well as having a fractured skull. He talked a lot of the selections and old John Tierney, of the old bark school; and the Never-Never country with Jack—and, later on, of the present. "What's Ben sayin' now, Jim?" asked one young bushman as another came out of the room with an awestruck face.

"He's sayin' that Jack Denver's dead, killed ridin' home from the races, an' that the funeral's to-morrow, an' we're to roll up at Talbragar!" answered the other, with wide eyes, a blank face and in an awed voice. "He's thinkin' to-day's yesterday."

But towards the end, under the ministrations of the doctor, Ben became conscious. He rolled his head a little on the pillow after he woke, and then, seeming to remember all that happened up to his stunning fall, he asked quietly:

"What sort of a funeral did Jack have?"

They told him it was the biggest ever seen in the district.

"Muster bin more'n a mile long," said one.

"Watcher talkin' about, Jim?" put in another. "Yer talkin' through yer socks. It was more'n a mile an' a half, Ben, if it was er inch. Some of the chaps timed it an' measured it an' compared notes as well as they could. Why, the head was at the Racecourse when the tail was at Old—"

Ben sank back satisfied and a little later took the track that Jack Denver had taken.

WANTED BY THE POLICE

Could it have been the Soul of Man and none higher that gave spoken and written word to the noblest precepts of human nature? For the deeper you sound it the more noble it seems, in spite of all the wrong, injustice, sin, sorrow, pain, religion, atheism, and cynics in the world. We make (or are supposed to make, or allow others to make) laws for the protection of society, or property, or religion, or what you will; and we pay thousands of men like ourselves to protect those laws and see them carried out; and we build and maintain expensive offices, police stations, court-houses and jails for the protecting and carrying out of those laws, and the punishing of men—like ourselves—who break them. Yet, in our heart of hearts we are antagonistic to most of the laws, and to the Law as a whole (which we regard as an ass), and to the police magistrates and the judges. And we hate lawyers and loathe spies, pimps, and informers of all descriptions and the hangman with all our soul. For the Soul of Man says: Thou shalt not refuse refuge to the outcast, and thou shalt not betray the wanderer.

And those who do it we make outcast.

So we form Prisoners' Aid Societies, and Prisoners' Defence Societies, and subscribe to them and praise them and love them and encourage them to protect or defend men from the very laws that we pay so dearly to maintain. And how many of us, in the case of a crime against property—and though the property be public and ours—would refuse tucker to the hunted man, and a night's shelter from the pouring rain and the scowling, haunting, threatening, and terrifying darkness? Or show the police in the morning the track the poor wretch had taken? I know I couldn't.

The Heart of Man says: Thou shalt not.

At country railway stations, where the trains stop for refreshments, when a prisoner goes up or down in charge of a policeman, a native delicacy prevents the local loafers from seeming to notice him; but at the last moment there is always some hand to thrust in a clay pipe and cake of tobacco, and maybe a bag of sandwiches to the policeman.

And, when a prisoner escapes, in the country at least—unless he be a criminal maniac in for a serious offence, and therefore a real danger to society—we all honestly hope that they won't catch him, and we don't hide it. And, if put in a corner, most of us would help them not to catch him.

The thing came down through the ages and survived through the dark Middle Ages, as all good things come down through the ages and survive through the blackest ages. The hunted man in the tree, or cave, or hole, and strangers creeping to him with food in the darkness, and in fear and trembling; though he was, as often happened, an enemy to their creed, country, or party. For he was outcast, and hungry, and a wanderer whom men sought to kill.

These were mostly poor people or peasants; but it was so with the rich and well-to-do in the bloody Middle Ages. The Catholic country gentleman helping the Protestant refugee to escape disguised as a manservant (or a maidservant), and the Protestant country gentleman doing likewise by a hunted Catholic in his turn, as the battles went. Rebel helping royalist, and royalist helping rebel. And always, here and there, down through those ages, the delicate girl standing with her back to a door and her arms outstretched across it, and facing, with flashing eyes, the soldiers of the king or of the church—or entertaining and bluffing them with beautiful lies—to give some poor hunted devil time to hide or escape, though she a daughter of royalists and the church, and he a rebel to his king and a traitor to his creed. For they sought to kill him.

There was sanctuary in those times, in the monkeries—and the churches, where the soldiers of the king dared not go, for fear of God. There has been sanctuary since, in London and other places, where His or Her Majesty's police dared not go because of the fear of man. The "Rocks" was really sanctuary, even in my time—also Woolloomooloo. Now the only sanctuary is the jail.

And, not so far away, my masters! Down close to us in history, and in Merrie England, during Judge Jeffreys's "Bloody Assize," which followed on the Monmouth rebellion and formed the blackest page in English history, "a worthy widow named Elizabeth Gaunt was burned alive at Tyburn, for having sheltered a wretch who himself gave evidence against her. She settled the fuel about herself with her own hands, so that the flames should reach her quickly; and nobly said, with her last breath, that she had obeyed the sacred command of God, to give refuge to the outcast and not to betray the wanderer." (Charles Dickens's History of England.)

Note, I am not speaking of rebel to rebel, or loyalist to loyalist, or comrade to comrade, or clansman to clansman in trouble—that goes without saying—but of man and woman to man and woman in trouble, the highest form of clannishness, the clannishness that embraces the whole of this wicked world—the Clan of Mankind!

French people often helped English prisoners of war to escape to the coast and across the water, and English people did likewise by the French; and none dared raise the cry of "traitors." It was the highest form of patriotism on both sides. And, by the way, it was, is, and shall always be the women who are first to pity and help the rebel refugee or the fallen enemy.

Succour thine enemy.

There must have been a lot of human kindness under the smothering, stifling cloud of the "System" and behind the iron clank and swishing "cat" strokes of brutality—a lot of soul light in the darkness of our dark past—a page that has long since been closed down—when innocent men and women were transported to shame, misery, and horror; when mere boys were sent out on suspicion of stealing a hare from the squire's preserves, and mere girls on suspicion of lifting a riband from the merchant's counter. But the many kindly and self-sacrificing and even noble things that free and honest settlers did, in those days of loneliness and hardship, for wretched runaway convicts and others, are closed down with the pages too. My old grandmother used to tell me tales, but—well, I don't suppose a wanted man (or a man that wasn't wanted, for that matter) ever turned away from her huts, far back in the wild bush, without a quart of coffee and a "feed" inside his hunted carcass, or went short of a bit of bread and meat to see him on, and a gruff but friendly hint, maybe, from the old man himself. And they were a type of the early settlers, she an English lady and the daughter of a clergyman. Ah! well—

Do you ever seem to remember things that you could not possibly remember? Something that happened in your mother's life, maybe, if you are a girl, or your father's, if you are a boy—that happened to your mother or father some years, perhaps, before you were born. I have many such haunting memories—as of having once witnessed a murder, or an attempt at murder, for instance, and once seeing a tree fall on a man—and as a child I had a memory of having been a man myself once before. But here is one of the pictures.

A hut in a dark gully; slab and stringy-bark, two rooms and a detached kitchen with the boys' room roughly partitioned off it. Big clay fire-place with a big log fire in it. The settler, or selector, and his wife; another man who might have been "uncle," and a younger woman who might have been "aunt;" two little boys and the baby. It was raining heavens hard outside, and the night was as black as pitch. The uncle was reading a report in a paper (that seemed to have come, somehow, a long way from somewhere) about two men who were wanted for sheep- and cattle-stealing in the district. I decidedly remember it was during the reign of the squatters in the nearer west. There came a great gust that shook the kitchen and caused the mother to take up the baby out of the rough gin-case cradle. The father took his pipe from his mouth and said: "Ah, well! poor devils." "I hope they're not out in a night like this, poor fellows," said the mother, rocking the child in her arms. "And I hope they'll never catch 'em," snapped her sister. "The squatters has enough."

"I wonder where poor Jim is?" the mother moaned, rocking the baby, and with two of those great, silent tears starting from her haggard eyes.

"Oh don't start about Jim again, Ellen," said her sister impatiently. "He can take care of himself. You were always rushing off to meet trouble half-way—time enough when they come, God knows."

"Now, look here, Ellen," put in Uncle Abe, soothingly, "he was up in Queensland doing well when we last heerd of him. Ain't yer never goin' to be satisfied?"

Jim was evidently another and a younger uncle, whose temperament from boyhood had given his family constant cause for anxiety.

The father sat smoking, resting his elbow on his knee, bunching up his brush of red whiskers, and looking into the fire—and back into his own foreign past in his own foreign land perhaps: and, it may be, thinking in his own language.

Silence and smoke for a while; then the mother suddenly straightened up and lifted a finger:

"Hush! What's that? I thought I heard someone outside."

"Old Poley coughin'," said Uncle Abe, after they'd listened a space. "She must be pretty bad—oughter give her a hot bran mash." (Poley was the best milker.)

"But I fancied I heard horses at the sliprails," said the mother.

"Old Prince," said Uncle Abe. "Oughter let him into the shed."

"Hush!" said the mother, "there's someone outside." There was a step, as of someone retreating after peeping through a crack in the door, but it was not old Poley's step; then, from farther off, a cough that was like old Poley's cough, but had a rack in it.

"See who it is, Peter," said the mother. Uncle Abe, who was dramatic and an ass, slipped the old double-barrelled muzzle-loader from its leathers on the wall and stood it in the far corner and sat down by it. The mother, who didn't seem to realize anything, frowned at him impatiently. The coughing fit started again. It was a man.

"Who's there? Anyone outside there?" said the settler in a loud voice.

"It's all right. Is the boss there? I want to speak to him," replied a voice with no cough in it. The tone was reassuring, yet rather strained, as if there had been an accident—or it might be a cautious policeman or bushranger reconnoitring.

"Better see what he wants, Peter," said his sister-in-law quietly. "Something's the matter—it may be the police."

Peter threw an empty bag over his shoulders, took the peg from the door, opened it and stepped out. The racking fit of coughing burst forth again, nearer. "That's a church-yarder!" commented Uncle Abe.

The settler came inside and whispered to the others, who started up, interested. The coughing started again outside. When the fit was over the mother said:

"Wait a minute till I get the boys out of the road and then bring them in." The boys were bundled into the end room and told to go to bed at once. They knelt up on the rough bed of slabs and straw mattress, instead, and applied eyes and ears to the cracks in the partition.

The mother called to the father, who had gone outside again.

"Tell them to come inside, Peter."

"Better bring the horses into the yard first and put them under the shed," said the father to the unknown outside in the rain and darkness. Clatter of sliprails let down and tired hoofs over them, and sliprails put up again; then they came in.

Wringing wet and apparently knocked up, a tall man with black curly hair and beard, black eyes and eyebrows that made his face seem the whiter; dressed in tweed coat, too small for him and short at the sleeves, strapped riding-pants, leggings, and lace-up boots, all sodden. The other a mere boy, beardless or clean shaven, figure and face of a native, but lacking in something; dressed like his mate—like drovers or stockmen. Arms and legs of riders, both of them; cabbage-tree hats in left hands—as though the right ones had to be kept ready for something (and looking like it)—pistol butts probably. The young man had a racking cough that seemed to wrench and twist his frame as the settler steered him to a seat on a stool by the fire. (In the intervals of coughing he glared round like a watched and hunted sneak-thief—as if the cough was something serious against the law, and he must try to stop it.)

"Take that wet coat off him at once, Peter," said the settler's wife, "and let me dry it." Then, on second thoughts: "Take this candle and take him into the house and get some dry things on him."

The dark man, who was still standing in the doorway, swung aside to let them pass as the settler steered the young man into the "house;" then swung back again. He stood, drooping rather, with one hand on the door-post; his big, wild, dark eyes kept glancing round and round the room and even at the ceiling, seeming to overlook or be unconscious of the faces after the first keen glance, but always coming back to rest on the door in the partition of the boys' room opposite.

"Won't you sit down by the fire and rest and dry yourself?" asked the settler's wife, rather timidly, after watching him for a moment.

He looked at the door again, abstractedly it seemed, or as if he had not heard her.

Then Uncle Abe (who, by the way, was supposed to know more than he should have been supposed to know) spoke out.

"Set down, man! Set down and dry yerself. There's no one there except the boys—that's the boys' room. Would yer like to look through?"

The man seemed to rouse himself from a reverie. He let his arm and hand fall from the doorpost to his side like dead things. "Thank you, missus," he said, apparently unconscious of Uncle Abe, and went and sat down in front of the fire.

"Hadn't you better take your wet coat off and let me dry it?"

"Thank you." He took off his coat, and, turning the sleeve, inside out, hung it from his knees with the lining to the fire then he leaned forward, with his hands on his knees, and stared at the burning logs and steam. He was unarmed, or, if not, had left his pistols in the saddle-bag outside.

Andy Page, general handy-man (who was there all the time, but has not been mentioned yet, because he didn't mention anything himself which seemed necessary to this dark picture), now remarked to the stranger, with a wooden-face expression but a soft heart, that the rain would be a good thing for the grass, mister, and make it grow; a safe remark to make under the present, or, for the matter of that, under any circumstances.

The stranger said, "Yes; it would."

"It will make it spring up like anything," said Andy.

The stranger admitted that it would.

Uncle Abe joined in, or, rather, slid in, and they talked about the drought and the rain and the state of the country, in monosyllables mostly, with "Jesso," and "So it is," and "You're right there," till the settler came back with the young man dressed in rough and patched, but dry, clothes. He took another stool by his mate's side at the fire, and had another fit of coughing. When it was over, Uncle Abe remarked "That's a regular church-yarder yer got, young feller."

The young fellow, too exhausted to speak, even had he intended doing so, turned his head in a quick, half-terrified way and gave it two short jerky nods.

The settler had brought a bottle out—it was gin they kept for medicine. They gave him some hot, and he took it in his sudden, frightened, half-animal way, like a dog that was used to ill-usage.

"He ought to be in the hospital," said the mother.

"He ought to be in bed right now at once," snapped the sister. "Couldn't you stay till morning, or at least till the rain clears up?" she said to the elder man. "No one ain't likely to come near this place in this weather."

"If we did he'd stand a good chance to get both hospital and a bed pretty soon, and for a long stretch, too," said the dark man grimly. "No, thank you all the same, miss—and missus—I'll get him fixed up all right and safe before morning."

The father came into the end room with a couple of small feed boxes and both boys tumbled under the blankets. The father emptied some chaff, from a bag in the corner, into the boxes, and then dished some corn from another bag into the chaff and mixed it well with his hands. Then he went out with the boxes under his arms, and the boys got up again.

The mother had brought two chairs from the front room (I remember the kind well: black painted hardwood that were always coming to pieces and with apples painted on the backs). She stood them with their backs to the fire and, taking up the young man's wet clothes, which the settler had brought out under his arm and thrown on a stool, arranged them over the backs of chairs and the stool to dry. He lost some of his nervousness or seared manner under the influence of the gin, and answered one or two questions with reference to his complaint.

The baby was in the cradle asleep. The sister drew boiling water from the old-fashioned fountain over one side of the fire and made coffee. The mother laid the coarse brownish cloth and set out the camp-oven bread, salt beef, tin plates, and pintpots. This was always called "setting the table" in the bush. "You'd better have it by the fire," said the bush-wife to the dark man.

"Thank you, missus," he said, as he moved to a bench by the table, "but it's plenty warm enough here. Come on, Jack."

Jack, under the influence of another tot, was in a fit state to sit down to a table something like a Christian, instead of coming to his food like a beaten dog.

The hum of bush common-places went on. One of the boys fell across the bed and into deep slumber; the other watched on awhile, but must have dozed.

When he was next aware, he saw, through the cracks, the taller man putting on his dried coat by the fire; then he went to a rough "sofa" at the side of the kitchen, where the young man was sleeping—with his head and shoulders curled in to the wall and his arm over his face, like a possum hiding from the light—and touched him on the shoulder.

"Come on, Jack," he said, "wake up."

Jack sprang to his feet with a blundering rush, grappled with his mate, and made a break for the door.

"It's all right, Jack," said the other, gently yet firmly, holding and shaking him. "Go in with the boss and get into your own clothes—we've got to make a start." The other came to himself and went inside quietly with the settler. The dark man stretched himself, crossed the kitchen and looked down at the sleeping child; he returned to the fire without comment. The wildness had left his eyes. The bushwoman was busy putting some tucker in a sugar-bag. "There's tea and sugar and salt in these mustard tins, and they won't get wet," she said, "and there's some butter too; but I don't know how you'll manage about the bread—I've wrapped it up, but you'll have to keep it dry as well as you can."

"Thank you, missus, but that'll be all right. I've got a bit of oil-cloth," he said.

They spoke lamely for a while, against time; then the bushwoman touched the spring, and their voices became suddenly low and earnest as they drew together. The stranger spoke as at a funeral, but the funeral was his own.

"I don't care about myself so much," he said, "for I'm tired of it, and—and—for the matter of that I'm tired of everything; but I'd like to see poor Jack right, and I'll try to get clear myself, for his sake. You've seen him. I can't blame myself, for I took him from a life that was worse than jail. You know how much worse than animals some brutes treat their children in the bush. And he was an 'adopted.' You know what that means. He was idiotic with ill-treatment when I got hold of him. He's sensible enough when away with me, and true as steel. He's about the only living human thing I've got to care for, or to care for me, and I want to win out of this hell for his sake."

He paused, and they were all silent. He was measuring time, as his next words proved: "Jack must be nearly ready now." Then he took a packet from some inside pocket of his blue dungaree shirt. It was wrapped in oil-cloth, and he opened it and laid it on the table; there was a small Bible and a packet of letters—and portraits, maybe.

"Now, missus," he said, "you mustn't think me soft, and I'm neither a religious man nor a hypocrite. But that Bible was given to me by my mother, and her hand-writing is in it, so I couldn't chuck it away. Some of the letters are hers and some—someone else's. You can read them if you like. Now, I want you to take care of them for me and dry them if they are a little damp. If I get clear I'll send for them some day, and, if I don't—well, I don't want them to be taken with me. I don't want the police to know who I was, and what I was, and who my relatives are and where they are. You wouldn't have known, if you do know now, only your husband knew me on the diggings, and happened to be in the court when I got off on that first cattle-stealing charge, and recognized me again to-night. I can't thank you enough, but I want you to remember that I'll never forget. Even if I'm taken and have to serve my time I'll never forget it, and I'll live to prove it."

"We—we don't want no thanks, an' we don't want no proofs," said the bushwoman, her voice breaking.

The sister, her eyes suspiciously bright, took up the packet in her sharp, practical way, and put it in a work-box she had in the kitchen.

The settler brought the young fellow out dressed in his own clothes. The elder shook hands quietly all round, or, rather, they shook hands with him. "Now, Jack!" he said. They had fastened an oilskin cape round Jack's shoulders.

Jack came forward and shook hands with a nervous grip that he seemed to have trouble to take off. "I won't forget it," he said; "that's all I can say—I won't forget it." Then they went out with the settler. The rain had held up a little. Clatter of sliprails down and up, but the settler didn't come back.

"Wonder what Peter's doing?" said the wife.

"Showin' 'em down the short cut," said Uncle Abe.

But, presently, clatter of sliprails down again, and cattle driven over them.

"Wonder what he's doing with the cows," said the wife.

They waited in wonder, and with growing anxiety, for some quarter of an hour; then Abe and Andy, going out to see, met the settler coming back.

"What in thunder are you doing with the cows, Peter?" asked Uncle Abe.

"Oh, just driving them out and along a bit over those horse tracks; we might get into trouble," said Peter.

When the boys woke it was morning, and the mother stood by the bed. "You needn't get up yet, and don't say anyone was here last night if you're asked," she whispered, and went out. They were up on their knees at once with their eyes to the cracks, and got the scare of their young lives. Three mounted troopers were steaming their legs at the fire—their bodies had been protected by oilskin capes. The mother was busy about the table and the sister changing the baby. Presently the two younger policemen sat down to bread and bacon and coffee, but their senior (the sergeant) stood with his back to the fire, with a pint-pot of coffee in his hand, eating nothing, but frowning suspiciously round the room.

Said one of the young troopers to Aunt Annie, to break the lowering silence, "You don't remember me?"

"Oh yes, I do; you were at Brown's School at Old Pipeclay—but I was only there a few months."

"You look as if you didn't get much sleep," said the senior-sergeant, bluntly, to the settler's wife, "and your sister too."

"And so would you," said Aunt Annie, sharply, "if you were up with a sick baby all night."

"Sad affair that, about Brown the schoolmaster," said the younger trooper to Aunt Annie.

"Yes," said Aunt Annie, "it was indeed."

The senior-sergeant stood glowering. Presently he said brutally—"The baby don't seem to be very sick; what's the matter with it?"

The young troopers move uneasily, and one impatiently.

"You should have seen her" (the baby) "about twelve o'clock last night," said Aunt Annie, "we never thought she would live till the morning."

"Oh, didn't you?" said the senior-sergeant, in a half-and-half tone.

The mother took the baby and held it so that its face was hidden from the elder policeman.

"What became of Brown's family, miss?" asked the young trooper. "Do you remember Lucy Brown?"

"I really don't know," answered Aunt Annie, "all I know is that they went to Sydney. But I think I heard that Lucy was married."

Just then Uncle Abe and Andy came in to breakfast. Andy sat down in the corner with a wooden face, and Uncle Abe, who was a tall man, took up a position, with his back to the fire, by the side of the senior trooper, and seemed perfectly at home and at ease. He lifted up his coat behind, and his face was a study in bucolic unconsciousness. The settler passed through to the boys' room (which was harness room, feed room, tool house, and several other things), and as he passed out with a shovel the sergeant said, "So you haven't seen anyone along here for three days?"

"No," said the settler.

"Except Jimmy Marshfield that took over Barker's selection in Long Gully," put in Aunt Annie. "He was here yesterday. Do you want him?"

"An' them three fellers on horseback as rode past the corner of the lower paddock the day afore yesterday," mumbled Uncle Abe, "but one of 'em was one of the Coxes' boys, I think."

At the sound of Uncle Abe's voice both women started and paled, and looked as if they'd like to gag him, but he was safe.

"What were they like?" asked the constable.

The women paled again, but Uncle Abe described them. He had imagination, and was only slow where the truth was concerned.

"Which way were they going?" asked the constable. "Towards Mudgee" (the police-station township), said Uncle Abe.

The constable gave his arm an impatient jerk and dropped Uncle Abe.

Uncle Abe looked as if he wanted badly to wink hard at someone, but there was no friendly eye in the line of wink that would be safe.

"Well, it's strange," said the sergeant, "that the men we're after didn't look up an out-of-the-way place like this for tucker, or horse-feed, or news, or something."

"Now, look here," said Aunt Annie, "we're neither cattle duffers nor sympathizers; we're honest, hard-working people, and God knows we're glad enough to see a strange face when it comes to this lonely hole; and if you only want to insult us, you'd better stop it at once. I tell you there's nobody been here but old Jimmy Marshfield for three days, and we haven't seen a stranger for over a fortnight, and that's enough. My sister's delicate and worried enough without you." She had a masculine habit of putting her hand up on something when holding forth, and as it happened it rested on the work-box on the shelf that contained the cattle-stealer's mother's Bible; but if put to it, Aunt Annie would have sworn on the Bible itself.

"Oh well, no offence, no offence," said the constable. "Come on, men, if you've finished, it's no use wasting time round here."

The two young troopers thanked the mother for their breakfast, and strange to say, the one who had spoken to her went up to Aunt Annie and shook hands warmly with her. Then they went out, and mounting, rode back in the direction of Mudgee. Uncle Abe winked long and hard and solemnly at Andy Page, and Andy winked back like a mechanical wooden image. The two women nudged and smiled and seemed quite girlish, not to say skittish, all the morning. Something had come to break the cruel hopeless monotony of their lives. And even the settler became foolishly cheerful.

Five years later: same hut, same yard, and a not much wider clearing in the gully, and a little more fencing—the women rather more haggard and tired looking, the settler rather more horny-handed and silent, and Uncle Abe rather more philosophical. The men had had to go out and work on the stations. With the settler and his wife it was, "If we only had a few pounds to get the farm cleared and fenced, and another good plough horse, and a few more cows." That had been the burden of their song for the five years and more.

Then, one evening, the mail boy left a parcel. It was a small parcel, in cloth-paper, carefully tied and sealed. What could it be? It couldn't be the Christmas number of a weekly they subscribed to, for it never came like that. Aunt Annie cut the discussion short by cutting the string with a table knife and breaking the wax.

And behold, a clean sugar-bag tightly folded and rolled.

And inside a strong whitey-brown envelope.

And on the envelope written or rather printed the words:

"For horse-feed, stabling, and supper."

And underneath, in smaller letters, "Send Bible and portraits to—." (Here a name and address.)

And inside the envelope a roll of notes.

"Count them," said Aunt Annie.

But the settler's horny and knotty hands trembled too much, and so did his wife's withered ones; so Aunt Annie counted them.

"Fifty pounds!" she said.

"Fifty pounds!" mused the settler, scratching his head in a perplexed way.

"Fifty pounds!" gasped his wife.

"Yes," said Aunt Annie sharply, "fifty pounds!"

"Well, you'll get it settled between yer some day!" drawled Uncle Abe.

Later, after thinking comfortably over the matter, he observed:

"Cast yer coffee an' bread an' bacon upon the waters—"

Uncle Abe never hurried himself or anybody else.

THE BATH

The moral should be revived. Therefore, this is a story with a moral. The lower end of Bill Street—otherwise William—overlooks Blue's Point Road, with a vacant wedge-shaped allotment running down from a Scottish church between Bill Street the aforesaid and the road, and a terrace on the other side of the road. A cheap, mean-looking terrace of houses, flush with the pavement, each with two windows upstairs and a large one in the middle downstairs, with a slit on one side of it called a door—looking remarkably skully in ghastly dawns, afterglows, and rainy afternoons and evenings. The slits look as if the owners of the skulls got it there from an upward blow of a sharp tomahawk, from a shorter man—who was no friend of theirs—just about the time they died. The slits open occasionally, and mothers of the nation, mostly holding their garments together at neck or bosom, lean out—at right angles almost—and peer up and down the road, as if they are casually curious as to what is keeping the rent collector so late this morning. Then they shut up till late in the day, when a boy or two comes home from work. The terrace should be called "Jim's Terrace" if the road is not "James's" Road, because no bills ever seem to be paid there as they are in our street—and for other reasons. There are four houses, but seldom more than two of them occupied at one time—often only one. Tenants never shift in, or at least are never seen to, but they get there. The sign is a furtive candle light behind an old table cloth, a skirt, or any rag of dark stuff tacked across the front bedroom window, upstairs, and a shadow suggestive of a woman making up a bed on the floor.

If more than two of the houses are occupied there is almost certain to be an old granny with ragged grey hair, who folded her arms tight under her ragged old breasts, and bends her tough old body, and sticks her ragged grey old head out of the slit called a door, and squints up and down the road, but not in the interests of mischief-making—they are never here long enough—only out of mild, ragged, grey-headed curiosity regarding the health or affairs of the rent collector.

Perhaps there are no bills to be collected in Skull Terrace because no credit is given. No jugs are put out, because there is no place to put them, except on the pavement, or on the narrow window ledges, where they would be in great and constant danger from the feet or elbows of passers-by. There are no tradesmen's entrances to the houses in Skull Terrace.

Tenants and sub-tenants often leave on Friday morning in the full glare of the day. Granny throws down garments from the top window to hurry things, and the wife below ties up much in an old allegedly green or red table-cloth, on the pavement, at the last moment. Van of the "bottle ho" variety. It is all done very quickly, and nobody takes any notice—they are never there long enough. Landlord, landlady, or rent collector—or whatever it is—calls later on; maybe, knocks in a tired, even bored, way; makes inquiries next door, and goes away, leaving the problem to take care of itself—all kind of casual. The business people of North Sydney, especially removers and labourers, are very casual. Down old Blue's Point Road the folk get so casual that they just exist, but don't seem to do so.

One thing I never could make out about Skull Terrace is that when one house becomes vacant from a house agent's point of view—there is a permanent atmosphere of vacancy about the whole terrace—the people of another move into it. And there's not the slightest difference between the houses. It is because the removal is such a small affair, I suppose, and the change is, the main thing. I always do better for awhile in a new house—but then I always did seem to get on better somewhere else.

There are many points, or absence of points, about Skull Terrace that fit in with Jim's casualness as against Bill's character, therefore Blue's Point Road ought to be James's Street.

But just now, in the heat of summer, the terrace happens to be full, and all the blinds are decent—the two new-comers are newly come down to Skull Terrace, and the other blinds are looked up, washed, and fixed up by force of example or from very shame's sake.

All of which seems to have nothing whatever to do with the story, except that the scene is down opposite my balcony as I think and smoke, and it is a blur on one of the most beautiful harbour views in the world.

I had been working hard all day, mending the fence, putting up a fowl-house and some lattice work and wire netting, and limewashing and painting. Labours of love. I'd rather build a fowl-house than a "pome" or story, any day. And when finished—the fowl-house, I mean—I sit and contemplate my handiwork with pure and unadulterated joy. And I take a candle out several times, after dark, to look at it again. I never got such pleasure out of rhyme, story, or first-class London Academy notice. I find it difficult to drag myself from the fowl-house, or whatever it is, to meals, and harder to this work, and I lie awake planning next day's work until I fall asleep in the sleep of utter happy weariness. And I'm up and at it, before washing, at daylight. But I was a carpenter and housepainter first.

Well, it had been a long, close day, and I was very dirty and tired, but with the energy and restlessness of healthy, happy tiredness when work is unfinished. But I was out of two-inch nails, and the shops were shut.

Then it struck me to start up the copper and have a real warm bath after my own heart and ideas. The bathroom is outside, next the wash-house and copper. There were plenty of splinters and ends of softwood that were mine by right of purchase and labour. My landlady is, and always has been, sensitive on the subject of firewood. She'll buy anything else to make the house comfortable and beautiful. She has been known to buy a piano for one of her nieces and burn rubbish in the stove the same day. I knew she was uneasy about the softwood odds and ends, but I couldn't help that—she'd still be sentimental about them if she had a stack of firewood as big as the house. There's at least one thing that most folk hate to buy—mine's boot-laces or bone studs, so long as I can make pins or inked string do.

I put a bucket of water in the copper, started a fire under that sent sparks out of the wash-house flue at an alarming rate, filled the copper to the brim, and, in the absence of a lid, covered it with a piece of flattened galvanized iron I had.

I tacked the side edge of a strip of canvas to the matchboard wall along over the inner edge of the bath, fastened a short piece of gas-pipe to the outer edge, with pieces of string through holes made in it, and let it hang down over the bath, leaving a hole at the head for my head and shoulders. I was going to have a long, comfortable, and utterly lazy and drowsy hot water and steam bath, you know.

I fastened a piece of clothes-line round and over the head of the bath, and twisted an old toilet-table cover and a towel round it where it sagged into the bath, for a head rest-also to be soaped for where I couldn't get at my back with my hands.

I went up to my room for some things, and it struck me to arrange two chairs by the bed—candle and matches and tobacco on one side, and a pile of Jack London, Kipling, and Yankee magazines on the other, with the last Lone Hand and Bulletin on top.

Going down with pyjamas, towel, and soap, it struck me to have a kettle and a saucepan full of water on the stove to use as the water from the copper cooled.

I took a roomy, hard-bottomed kitchen chair into the bathroom; on it I placed a carefully scraped, cleared, and filled pipe, matches, more tobacco, tooth-brush, saucer with a lump of whiting and salt, piece of looking-glass—to see progress of the teeth—and knife for finger and toe nails. And I knocked up a few three-inch iron nails in the wall to hang things on. I placed a clean suit of pyjamas over the back of the chair, and over them the towels.

I arranged with the landlady to have a good cup of coffee made, as she knows how to make it, ready to hand in round the edge of the door when I should be in the bath. There's nothing in that. I've been with her for years, and on account of the canvas it would be just the same as if I were in bed. On second thought I asked her to hand in some toast—or bread and butter and bloater paste—at the same time. I fed the fire with judgment, and the copper boiled just as the last blaze died down. I got a pail and carried the water to the bath, pouring it in through the opening at the head. The last few pints I dipped into the pail with a cup. I covered the opening with a towel to keep the steam and heat in until I was ready. I got the boiling water from the kitchen into the bucket, covered it with another towel, and stood it in a handy corner in the bathroom.

I made an opening, turned on the cold water, and commenced to undress. I hung my clothes on the wall, till morning, for I intended to go straight from the bath to bed in my pyjamas and to lie there reading.

I turned off the cold water tap to be sure, lifted the towel off, and put my good right foot in to feel the temperature—into about three inches of cold water, and that was vanishing.

I'd forgotten to put in the plug.

I'm deaf, you know, and the landlady, hearing the water run, thought I was flushing out the bath (we were new tenants) and wondered vaguely why I was so long at it.

I dressed rather hurriedly in my working clothes, went inside, and spread myself dramatically on the old cane lounge and covered my face with my oldest hat, to show that it was comic and I took it that way. But my landlady was so full of sympathy, condolence, and self-reproach (because she failed to draw my attention to the gurgling) that she let the coffee and toast burn.

I went up and lay on my bed, and was so tired and misty and far away that I went to sleep without undressing, or even washing my face and hands.

How many, in this life, forget the plug!

And how many, ah! how many, who passed through, and are passing through Skull Terrace, commenced life as confidently, carefree, and clear headed, and with such easily exercised, careful, intelligent, practised, and methodical attention to details as I did the bath business arrangements—and forgot to put in the plug.

And many because they were handicapped physically.

INSTINCT GONE WRONG

Old Mac used to sleep in his wagon in fine weather, when he had no load, on his blankets spread out on the feed-bags; but one time he struck Croydon, flush from a lucky and good back trip, and looked in at the (say) Royal Hotel to wet his luck—as some men do with their sorrow—and he "got there all right." Next morning he had breakfast in the dining-room, was waited on as a star boarder, and became thoroughly demoralized; and his mind was made up (independent of himself, as it were) to be a gentleman for once in his life. He went over to the store and bought the sloppiest suit of reach-me-downs of glossiest black, and the stiffest and stickiest white shirt they had to show—also four bone studs, two for the collar and two for the cuffs. Then he gave his worn "larstins" to the stable-boy (with half a crown) to clean, and—proceeded. He put the boots on during the day, one at a time between drinks, gassing all the time, and continued. He concluded about midnight, after a very noisy time and interviews with everyone on sight (slightly interrupted by drinks) concerning "his room." It was show time, you see, and all the rooms were as full as he was—he was too full even to share the parlour or billiard room with others; but he consented at last to a shake-down on the balcony, the barmaid volunteering to spread the couch with her own fair hands.

Towards daylight he woke, for one of the reasons why men do wake. It is well known, to people who know, that old campers-out (and young men new to it, too) will wake once—if in a party, each at different times—to tend to their cattle, or listen for the hobbles of their horses, or simply to rise on their elbows and have a look round—the last, I suppose, from an instinct born in old dangerous times. Mac woke up, and it was dark. He reached out and his hand fell, instinctively, on the rail of the balcony, which was to him (instinctively—and that shows how instinct errs) the rail of the side of his wagon, in which as I have said, he was wont to sleep. So he drew himself up on his knees and to his feet, with the instinctive intention of getting down to (say) put some chaff and corn in the feed-bags stretched across the shafts for the horses; for he intended, by instinct, to make an early start. Which shows how instinct can never be trusted to travel with memory, but will get ahead of it—or behind it. (Say it was instinct mixed with or adulterated by drink.) He got a long, hairy leg over and felt (instinctively) for the hub of the wheel; his foot found and rested on the projecting ledge of the balcony floor outside, and that, to him, was the hub all right. He swung his other leg over and expected to drop lightly on to the grass or dust of the camp; but, being instinctively rigid, he fell heavily some fifteen feet into a kerbed gutter.

As a result of his howls lights soon flickered in windows and fanlights; and with prompt, eager, anxious, and awed bush first-aid and assistance, they carried a very sober, battered and blasphemous driver inside and spread mattresses on the floor. And, some six weeks afterwards, an image, mostly of plaster-of-Paris and bandages, reclined, much against its will, on a be-cushioned cane lounge on the hospital veranda; and, from the only free and workable corner of its mouth, when the pipe was removed, came shockingly expressed opinions of them—newfangled—two-story—! "night houses" (as it called them). And, thereafter, when he had a load on, or the weather was too bad for sleeping in or under his wagon, the veranda of a one-storied shanty (if he could get to it) was good enough for MacSomething, the carrier.

THE HYPNOTIZED TOWNSHIP

They said that Harry Chatswood, the mail contractor would do anything for Cobb & Co., even to stretching fencing-wire across the road in a likely place: but I don't believe that—Harry was too good-hearted to risk injuring innocent passengers, and he had a fellow feeling for drivers, being an old coach driver on rough out-back tracks himself. But he did rig up fencing-wire for old Mac, the carrier, one night, though not across the road. Harry, by the way, was a city-born bushman, who had been everything for some years. Anything from six-foot-six to six-foot-nine, fourteen stone, and a hard case. He is a very successful coach-builder now, for he knows the wood, the roads, and the weak parts in a coach.

It was in the good seasons when competition was keen and men's hearts were hard—not as it is in times of drought, when there is no competition, and men's hearts are soft, and there is all kindness and goodwill between them. He had had much opposition in fighting Cobb & Co., and his coaches had won through on the outer tracks. There was little malice in his composition, but when old Mac, the teamster, turned his teams over to his sons and started a light van for parcels and passengers from Cunnamulla—

that place which always sounds to me suggestive of pumpkin pies—out in seeming opposition to Harry Chatswood, Harry was annoyed.

Perhaps Mac only wished to end his days on the road with parcels that were light and easy to handle (not like loads of fencing wire) and passengers that were sociable; but he had been doing well with his teams, and, besides, Harry thought he was after the mail contract: so Harry was annoyed more than he was injured. Mac was mean with the money he had not because of the money he had a chance of getting; and he mostly slept in his van, in all weathers, when away from home which was kept by his wife about half-way between the half-way house and the next "township."

One dark, gusty evening, Harry Chatswood's coach dragged, heavily though passengerless, into Cunnamulla, and, as he turned into the yard of the local "Royal," he saw Mac's tilted four-wheeler (which he called his "van") drawn up opposite by the kerbing round the post office. Mac always chose a central position—with a vague idea of advertisement perhaps. But the nearness to the P.O. reminded Harry of the mail contracts, and he knew that Mac had taken up a passenger or two and some parcels in front of him (Harry) on the trip in. And something told Harry that Mac was asleep inside his van. It was a windy night, with signs of rain, and the curtains were drawn close.

Old Mac was there all right, and sleeping the sleep of a tired driver after a long drowsy day on a hard box-seat, with little or no back railing to it. But there was a lecture on, or an exhibition of hypnotism or mesmerism—"a blanky spirit rappin' fake," they called it, run by "some blanker" in "the hall;" and when old Mac had seen to his horses, he thought he might as well drop in for half an hour and see what was going on. Being a Mac, he was, of course, theological, scientific, and argumentative. He saw some things which woke him up, challenged the performer to hypnotize him, was "operated" on or "fooled with" a bit, had a "numb sorter light-headed feelin'," and was told by a voice from the back of the hall that his "leg was being pulled, Mac," and by another buzzin' far-away kind of "ventrillick" voice that he would make a good subject, and that, if he only had the will power and knew how (which he would learn from a book the professor had to sell for five shillings) he would be able to drive his van without horses or any thing, save the pole sticking straight out in front. These weren't the professor's exact words—But, anyway, Mae came to himself with a sudden jerk, left with a great Scottish snort of disgust and the sound of heavy boots along the floor; and after a resentful whisky at the Royal, where they laughed at his scrooging bushy eyebrows, fierce black eyes and his deadly-in-earnest denunciation of all humbugs and imposters, he returned to the aforesaid van, let down the flaps, buttoned the daft and "feekle" world out, and himself in, and then retired some more and slept, as I have said, rolled in his blankets and overcoats on a bed of cushions, and chaff-bag.

Harry Chatswood got down from his empty coach, and was helping the yard boy take out the horses, when his eye fell on the remnant of a roll of fencing wire standing by the stable wall in the light of the lantern. Then an idea struck him unexpectedly, and his mind became luminous. He unhooked the swinglebar, swung it up over his "leader's" rump (he was driving only three horses that trip), and hooked it on to the horns of the hames. Then he went inside (there was another light there) and brought out a bridle and an old pair of spurs that were hanging on the wall. He buckled on the spurs at the chopping block, slipped the winkers off the leader and the bridle on, and took up the fencing-wire, and started out the gate with the horse. The boy gaped after him once, and then hurried to put up the other two horses. He knew Harry Chatswood, and was in a hurry to see what he would be up to.

There was a good crowd in town for the show, or the races, or a stock sale, or land ballot, or something; but most of them were tired, or at tea—or in the pubs—and the corners were deserted. Observe how fate makes time and things fit when she wants to do a good turn—or play a practical joke. Harry Chatswood, for instance, didn't know anything about the hypnotic business.

It was the corners of the main street or road and the principal short cross street, and the van was opposite the pub stables in the main street. Harry crossed the streets diagonally to the opposite corner, in a line with the van. There he slipped the bar down over the horse's rump, and fastened one end of the wire on to the ring of it. Then he walked back to the van, carrying the wire and letting the coils go wide, and, as noiselessly as possible, made a loop in the loose end and slipped it over the hooks on the end of the pole. ("Unnecessary detail!" my contemporaries will moan, "Overloaded with uninteresting details!" But that's because they haven't got the details—and it's the details that go.) Then Harry skipped back to his horse, jumped on, gathered up the bridle reins, and used his spurs. There was a swish and a clang, a scrunch and a clock-clock and rattle of wheels, and a surprised human sound; then a bump and a shout—for there was no underground drainage, and the gutters belonged to the Stone Age. There was a swift clocking and rattle, more shouts, another bump, and a yell. And so on down the longish main street. The stable-boy, who had left the horses in his excitement, burst into the bar, shouting, "The Hypnertism's on, the Mesmerism's on! Ole Mae's van's runnin' away with him without no horses all right!" The crowd scuffled out into the street; there were some unfortunate horses hanging up of course at the panel by the pub trough, and the first to get to them jumped on and rode; the rest ran. The hall—where they were clearing the willing professor out in favour of a "darnce"—and the other pubs decanted their contents, and chance souls skipped for the verandas of weather-board shanties out of which other souls popped to see the runaway. They saw a weird horseman, or rather, something like a camel (for Harry rode low, like Tod Sloan with his long back humped—for effect)—apparently fleeing for its life in a veil of dust, along the long white road, and some forty rods behind, an unaccountable tilted coach careered in its own separate cloud of dust. And from it came the shouts and yells. Men shouted and swore, women screamed for their children, and kids whimpered. Some of the men turned with an oath and stayed the panic with:

"It's only one of them flamin' motor-cars, you fools."

It might have been, and the yells the warning howls of a motorist who had burst or lost his honk-kook and his head.

"It's runnin' away!" or "The toff's mad or drunk!" shouted others. "It'll break its crimson back over the bridge."

"Let it!" was the verdict of some. "It's all the crimson carnal things are good for."

But the riders still rode and the footmen ran. There was a clatter of hoofs on the short white bridge looming ghostly ahead, and then, at a weird interval, the rattle and rumble of wheels, with no hoof-beats accompanying. The yells grew fainter. Harry's leader was a good horse, of the rather heavy coachhorse breed, with a little of the racing blood in her, but she was tired to start with, and only excitement and fright at the feel of the "pull" of the twisting wire kept her up to that speed; and now she was getting winded, so half a mile or so beyond the bridge Harry thought it had gone far enough, and he stopped and got down. The van ran on a bit, of course, and the loop of the wire slipped off the hooks of the pole. The wire recoiled itself roughly along the dust nearly to the heels of Harry's horse. Harry grabbed up as much of the wire as he could claw for, took the mare by the neck with the other hand, and vanished through the dense fringe of scrub off the road, till the wire caught and pulled him up; he stood still for a moment, in the black shadow on the edge of a little clearing, to listen. Then he fumbled with the wire until he got it untwisted, cast it off, and moved off silently with the mare across the soft rotten ground, and left her in a handy bush stockyard, to be brought back to the stables at a late hour that night—or rather an early hour next morning—by a jackaroo stable-boy who would have two half-crowns in his pocket and afterthought instructions to look out for that wire and hide it if possible.

Then Harry Chatswood got back quickly, by a roundabout way, and walked into the bar of the Royal, through the back entrance from the stables, and stared, and wanted to know where all the chaps had gone to, and what the noise was about, and whose trap had run away, and if anybody was hurt.

The growing crowd gathered round the van, silent and awestruck, and some of them threw off their hats, and lost them, in their anxiety to show respect for the dead, or render assistance to the hurt, as men do, round a bad accident in the bush. They got the old man out, and two of them helped him back along the road, with great solicitude, while some walked round the van, and swore beneath their breaths, or stared at it with open mouths, or examined it curiously, with their eyes only, and in breathless silence. They muttered, and agreed, in the pale moonlight now showing, that the sounds of the horses' hoofs had only been "spirit-rappin' sounds;" and, after some more muttering, two of the stoutest, with subdued oaths, laid hold of the pole and drew the van to the side of the road, where it would be out of the way of chance night traffic. But they stretched and rubbed their arms afterwards, and then, and on the way back, they swore to admiring acquaintances that they felt the "blanky 'lectricity" runnin' all up their arms and "elbers" while they were holding the pole, which, doubtless, they did—in imagination.

They got old Mac back to the Royal, with sundry hasty whiskies on the way. He was badly shaken, both physically, mentally, and in his convictions, and, when he'd pulled himself together, he had little to add to what they already knew. But he confessed that, when he got under his possum rug in the van, he couldn't help thinking of the professor and his creepy (it was "creepy," or "uncanny," or "awful," or "rum" with 'em now)—his blanky creepy hypnotism; and he (old Mac) had just laid on his back comfortable, and stretched his legs out straight, and his arms down straight by his sides, and drew long, slow breaths; and tried to fix his mind on nothing—as the professor had told him when he was "operatin' on him" in the hall. Then he began to feel a strange sort of numbness coming over him, and his limbs went heavy as lead, and he seemed to be gettin' light-headed. Then, all on a sudden, his arms seemed to begin to lift, and just when he was goin' to pull 'em down the van started as they had heard and seen it. After a while he got on to his knees and managed to wrench a corner; of the front curtain clear of the button and get his head out. And there was the van going helter-skelter, and feeling like Tam o'Shanter's mare (the old man said), and he on her barebacked. And there was no horses, but a cloud of dust—or a spook—on ahead, and the bare pole steering straight for it, just as the professor had said it would be. The old man thought he was going to be taken clear across the Never-Never country and left to roast on a sandhill, hundreds of miles from anywhere, for his sins, and he said he was trying to think of a prayer or two all the time he was yelling. They handed him more whisky from the publican's own bottle. Hushed and cautious inquiries for the Professor (with a big P now) elicited the hushed and cautious fact that he had gone to bed. But old Mac caught the awesome name and glared round, so they hurriedly filled out another for him, from the boss's bottle. Then there was a slight commotion. The housemaid hurried scaredly in to the bar behind and whispered to the boss. She had been startled nearly out of her wits by the Professor suddenly appearing at his bedroom door and calling upon her to have a stiff nobbler of whisky hot sent up to his room. The jackaroo yard-boy, aforesaid, volunteered to take it up, and while he was gone there were hints of hysterics from the kitchen, and the boss whispered in his turn to the crowd over the bar. The jackaroo just handed the tray and glass in through the partly opened door, had a glimpse of pyjamas, and, after what seemed an interminable wait, he came tiptoeing into the bar amongst its awe-struck haunters with an air of great mystery, and no news whatever.

They fixed old Mac on a shake-down in the Commercial Room, where he'd have light and some overflow guests on the sofas for company. With a last whisky in the bar, and a stiff whisky by his side on the floor, he was understood to chuckle to the effect that he knew he was all right when he'd won "the keystone o' the brig." Though how a wooden bridge with a level plank floor could have a keystone I don't know— and they were too much impressed by the event of the evening to inquire. And so, with a few cases of hysterics to occupy the attention of the younger women, some whimpering of frightened children and comforting or chastened nagging by mothers, some unwonted prayers muttered secretly and forgettingly, and a good deal of subdued blasphemy, Cunnamulla sank to its troubled slumbers—some of the sleepers in the commercial and billiard-rooms and parlours at the Royal, to start up in a cold sweat, out of their beery and hypnotic nightmares, to find Harry Chatswood making elaborate and fearsome passes over them with his long, gaunt arms and hands, and a flaming red table-cloth tied round his neck.

To be done with old Mac, for the present. He made one or two more trips, but always by daylight, taking care to pick up a swagman or a tramp when he had no passenger; but his "conveections" had had too much of a shaking, so he sold his turnout (privately and at a distance, for it was beginning to be called "the haunted van") and returned to his teams—always keeping one of the lads with him for company. He reckoned it would take the devil's own hypnotism to move a load of fencingwire, or pull a wool-team of bullocks out of a bog; and before he invoked the ungodly power, which he let them believe he could—he'd stick there and starve till he and his bullocks died a "natural" death. (He was a bit Irish—as all Scots are—back on one side.)

But the strangest is to come. The Professor, next morning, proved uncomfortably unsociable, and though he could have done a roaring business that night—and for a week of nights after, for that matter—and though he was approached several times, he, for some mysterious reason known only to himself, flatly refused to give one more performance, and said he was leaving the town that day. He couldn't get a vehicle of any kind, for fear, love, or money, until Harry Chatswood, who took a day off, volunteered, for a stiff consideration, to borrow a buggy and drive him (the Professor) to the next town towards the then railway terminus, in which town the Professor's fame was not so awesome, and where he might get a lift to the railway. Harry ventured to remark to the Professor once or twice during the drive that "there was a rum business with old Mac's van last night," but he could get nothing out of him, so gave it best, and finished the journey in contemplative silence.

Now, the fact was that the Professor had been the most surprised and startled man in Cunnamulla that night; and he brooded over the thing till he came to the conclusion that hypnotism was a dangerous power to meddle with unless a man was physically and financially strong and carefree—which he wasn't. So he threw it up.

He learnt the truth, some years later, from a brother of Harry Chatswood, in a Home or Retreat for Geniuses, where "friends were paying," and his recovery was so sudden that it surprised and disappointed the doctor and his friend, the manager of the home. As it was, the Professor had some difficulty in getting out of it.

Harry Chatswood, mail contractor (and several other things), was driving out from, say, Georgeville to Croydon, with mails, parcels, and only one passenger—a commercial traveller, who had shown himself unsociable, and close in several other ways. Nearly half-way to a place that was half-way between the halfway house and the town, Harry overhauled "Old Jack," a local character (there are many well-known characters named "Old Jack") and gave him a lift as a matter of course.

"Hello! Is that you, Jack?" in the gathering dusk.

"Yes, Harry."

"Then jump up here."

Harry was good-natured and would give anybody a lift if he could.

Old Jack climbed up on the box-seat, between Harry and the traveller, who grew rather more stand—(or rather sit) offish, wrapped himself closer in his overcoat, and buttoned his cloak of silence and general disgust to the chin button. Old Jack got his pipe to work and grunted, and chatted, and exchanged bush compliments with Harry comfortably. And so on to where they saw the light of a fire outside a hut ahead.

"Let me down here, Harry," said Old Jack uneasily, "I owe Mother Mac fourteen shillings for drinks, and I haven't got it on me, and I've been on the spree back yonder, and she'll know it, an' I don't want to face her. I'll cut across through the paddock and you can pick me up on the other side."

Harry thought a moment.

"Sit still, Jack," he said. "I'll fix that all right."

He twisted and went down into his trouser-pocket, the reins in one hand, and brought up a handful of silver. He held his hand down to the coach lamp, separated some of the silver from the rest by a sort of sleight of hand—or rather sleight of fingers—and handed the fourteen shillings over to Old Jack.

"Here y'are, Jack. Pay me some other time."

"Thanks, Harry!" grunted Old Jack, as he twisted for his pocket.

It was a cold night, the hint of a possible shanty thawed the traveller a bit, and he relaxed with a couple of grunts about the weather and the road, which were received in a brotherly spirit. Harry's horses stopped of their own accord in front of the house, an old bark-and-slab whitewashed humpy of the early settlers' farmhouse type, with a plank door in the middle, one bleary-lighted window on one side, and one forbiddingly blind one, as if death were there, on the other. It might have been. The door opened, letting out a flood of lamp-light and firelight which blindly showed the sides of the coach and the near pole horse and threw the coach lamps and the rest into the outer darkness of the opposing bush.

"Is that you, Harry?" called a voice and tone like Mrs Warren's of the Profession.

"It's me."

A stoutly aggressive woman appeared. She was rather florid, and looked, moved and spoke as if she had been something in the city in other years, and had been dumped down in the bush to make money in mysterious ways; had married, mated—or got herself to be supposed to be married—for convenience, and continued to make money by mysterious means. Anyway, she was "Mother Mac" to the bush, but, in the bank in the "town," and in the stores where she dealt, she was Mrs Mac, and there was always a promptly propped chair for her. She was, indeed, the missus of no other than old Mac, the teamster of hypnotic fame, and late opposition to Harry Chatswood. Hence, perhaps, part of Harry's hesitation to pull up, farther back, and his generosity to Old Jack.

Mrs or Mother Mac sold refreshments, from a rough bush dinner at eighteenpence a head to passengers, to a fly-blown bottle of ginger-ale or lemonade, hot in hot weather from a sunny fly-specked window. In between there was cold corned beef, bread and butter, and tea, and (best of all if they only knew it) a good bush billy of coffee on the coals before the fire on cold wet nights. And outside of it all, there was cold tea, which, when confidence was established, or they knew one of the party, she served hushedly in cups without saucers; for which she sometimes apologized, and which she took into her murderous bedroom to fill, and replenish, in its darkest and most felonious corner from homicidal-looking pots, by candle-light. You'd think you were in a cheap place, where you shouldn't be, in the city.

Harry and his passengers got down and stretched their legs, and while Old Jack was guardedly answering a hurriedly whispered inquiry of the traveller, Harry took the opportunity to nudge Mrs Mac, and whisper in her ear:

"Look out, Mrs Mac!—Exciseman!"

"The devil he is!" whispered she.

"Ye-e-es!" whispered Harry.

"All right, Harry!" she whispered. "Never a word! I'll take care of him, bless his soul."

After a warm at the wide wood fire, a gulp of coffee and a bite or two at the bread and meat, the traveller, now thoroughly thawed, stretched himself and said:

"Ah, well, Mrs Mac, haven't you got anything else to offer us?"

"And what more would you be wanting?" she snapped. "Isn't the bread and meat good enough for you?"

"But—but—you know—" he suggested lamely.

"Know?—I know!—What do I know?" A pause, then, with startling suddenness, "Phwat d'y' mean?"

"No offence, Mrs Mac—no offence; but haven't you got something in the way of—of a drink to offer us?"

"Dhrink! Isn't the coffee good enough for ye? I paid two and six a pound for ut, and the milk new from the cow this very evenin'—an' th' water rain-water."

"But—but—you know what I mean, Mrs Mac."

"An' I doan't know what ye mean. Phwat do ye mean? I've asked ye that before. What are ye dhrivin' at, man—out with it!"

"Well, I mean a little drop of the right stuff," he said, nettled. Then he added: "No offence—no harm done."

"O-o-oh!" she said, illumination bursting in upon her brain. "It's the dirrty drink ye're afther, is it? Well, I'll tell ye, first for last, that we doan't keep a little drop of the right stuff nor a little drop of the wrong stuff in this house. It's a honest house, an' me husband's a honest harrd-worrkin' carrier, as he'd soon let ye know if he was at home this cold night, poor man. No dirrty drink comes into this house, nor goes out of it, I'd have ye know."

"Now, now, Mrs Mac, between friends, I meant no offence; but it's a cold night, and I thought you might keep a bottle for medicine—or in case of accident—or snake-bite, you know—they mostly do in the bush."

"Medicine! And phwat should we want with medicine? This isn't a five-guinea private hospital. We're clean, healthy people, I'd have ye know. There's a bottle of painkiller, if that's what ye want, and a packet of salts left—maybe they'd do ye some good. An' a bottle of eye-water, an' something to put in your ear for th' earache—maybe ye'll want 'em both before ye go much farther."

"But, Mrs Mac—"

"No, no more of it!" she said. "I tell ye that if it's a nip ye're afther, ye'll have to go on fourteen miles to the pub in the town. Ye're coffee's gittin' cowld, an' it's eighteenpence each to passengers I charge on a night like this; Harry Chatswood's the driver an' welcome, an' Ould Jack's an ould friend." And she flounced round to clatter her feelings amongst the crockery on the dresser—just as men make a great show of filling and lighting their pipes in the middle of a barney. The table, by the way, was set on a brown holland cloth, with the brightest of tin plates for cold meals, and the brightest of tin pint-pots for the coffee (the crockery was in reserve for hot meals and special local occasions) and at one side of the wide fire-place hung an old-fashioned fountain, while in the other stood a camp-oven; and billies and a black kerosene-tin hung evermore over the fire from sooty chains. These, and a big bucket-handled frying-pan and a few rusty convict-time arms on the slab walls, were mostly to amuse jackaroos and jackarooesses, and let them think they were getting into the Australian-dontcherknow at last.

Harry Chatswood took the opportunity (he had a habit of taking opportunities of this sort) to whisper to Old Jack:

"Pay her the fourteen bob, Jack, and have done with it. She's got the needle to-night all right, and damfiknow what for. But the sight of your fourteen bob might bring her round." And Old Jack—as was his way—blundered obediently and promptly right into the hole that was shown him.

"Well, Mrs Mae," he said, getting up from the table and slipping his hand into his pocket. "I don't know what's come over yer to-night, but, anyway—" Here he put the money down on the table. "There's the money I owe yer for—for—"

"For what?" she demanded, turning on him with surprising swiftness for such a stout woman.

"The—the fourteen bob I owed for them drinks when Bill Hogan and me—"

"You don't owe me no fourteen bob for dhrinks, you dirty blaggard! Are ye mad? You got no drink off of me. Phwat d'ye mean?"

"Beg—beg pardin, Mrs Mac," stammered Old Jack, very much taken aback; "but the—yer know—the fourteen bob, anyway, I owed you when—that night when me an' Bill Hogan an' yer sister-in-law, Mary Don—"

"What? Well, I—Git out of me house, ye low blaggard! I'm a honest, respictable married woman, and so is me sister-in-law, Mary Donelly; and to think!—Git out of me door!" and she caught up the billy of coffee. "Git outside me door, or I'll let ye have it in ye'r ugly face, ye low woolscourer—an' it's nearly bilin'."

Old Jack stumbled dazedly out, and blind instinct got him on to the coach as the safest place. Harry Chatswood had stood with his long, gaunt figure hung by an elbow to the high mantelshelf, all the time, taking alternate gulps from his pint of coffee and puffs from his pipe, and very calmly and restfully regarding the scene.

"An' now," she said, "if the gentleman's done, I'd thank him to pay—it's eighteenpence—an' git his overcoat on. I've had enough dirty insults this night to last me a lifetime. To think of it—the blaggard!" she said to the table, "an' me a woman alone in a place like this on a night like this!"

The traveller calmly put down a two-shilling piece, as if the whole affair was the most ordinary thing in the world (for he was used to many bush things) and comfortably got into his overcoat.

"Well, Mrs Mae, I never thought Old Jack was mad before," said Harry Chatswood. "And I hinted to him," he added in a whisper. "Anyway" (out loudly), "you'll lend me a light, Mrs Mac, to have a look at that there swingle-bar of mine?"

"With pleasure, Harry," she said, "for you're a white man, anyway. I'll bring ye a light. An' all the lights in heaven if I could, an'—an' in the other place if they'd help ye."

When he'd looked to the swingle-bar, and had mounted to his place and untwisted the reins from a side-bar, she cried:

"An' as for them two, Harry, shpill them in the first creek you come to, an' God be good to you! It's all they're fit for, the low blaggards, to insult an honest woman alone in the bush in a place like this."

"All right, Mrs Mac," said Harry, cheerfully. "Good night, Mrs Mac."

"Good night, Harry, an' God go with ye, for the creeks are risen after last night's storm." And Harry drove on and left her to think over it.

She thought over it in a way that would have been unexpected to Harry, and would have made him uneasy, for he was really good-natured. She sat down on a stool by the fire, and presently, after thinking over it a bit, two big, lonely tears rolled down the lonely woman's fair, fat, blonde cheeks in the firelight.

"An' to think of Old Jack," she said. "The very last man in the world I'd dreamed of turning on me. But— but I always thought Old Jack was goin' a bit ratty, an' maybe I was a bit hard on him. God forgive us all!"

Had Harry Chatswood seen her then he would have been sorry he did it. Swagmen and broken-hearted new chums had met worse women than Mother Mac.

But she pulled herself together, got up and bustled round. She put on more wood, swept the hearth, put a parcel of fresh steak and sausages—brought by the coach—on to a clean plate on the table, and got some potatoes into a dish; for Chatswood had told her that her first and longest and favourite stepson was not far behind him with the bullock team. Before she had finished the potatoes she heard the clock-clock of heavy wheels and the crack of the bullock whip coming along the dark bush track.

But the very next morning a man riding back from Croydon called, and stuck his head under the veranda eaves with a bush greeting, and she told him all about it.

He straightened up, and tickled the back of his head with his little finger, and gaped at her for a minute.

"Why," he said, "that wasn't no excise officer. I know him well—I was drinking with him at the Royal last night afore we went to bed, an' had a nip with him this morning afore we started. Why! that's Bobby Howell, Burns and Bridges' traveller, an' a good sort when he wakes up, an' willin' with the money when he does good biz, especially when there's a chanst of a drink on a long road on a dark night."

"That Harry Chatswood again! The infernal villain," she cried, with a jerk of her arm. "But I'll be even with him, the dirrty blaggard. An' to think—I always knew Old Jack was a white man an'—to think! There's fourteen shillin's gone that Old Jack would have paid me, an' the traveller was good for three shillin's f'r the nips, an'—but Old Jack will pay me next time, and I'll be even with Harry Chatswood, the dirrty mail carter. I'll take it out of him in parcels—I'll be even with him."

She never saw Old Jack again with fourteen shillings, but she got even with Harry Chatswood, and—But I'll tell you about that some other time. Time for a last smoke before we turn in.

MATESHIP IN SHAKESPEARE'S ROME

How we do misquote sayings, or misunderstand them when quoted rightly! For instance, we "wait for something to turn up, like Micawber," careless or ignorant of the fact that Micawber worked harder than all the rest put together for the leading characters' sakes; he was the chief or only instrument in straightening out of the sadly mixed state of things—and he held his tongue till the time came. Moreover—and "Put a pin in that spot, young man," as Dr "Yark" used to say—when there came a turn in the tide of the affairs of Micawber, he took it at the flood, and it led on to fortune. He became a hardworking settler, a pioneer—a respected early citizen and magistrate in this bright young Commonwealth of ours, my masters!

And, by the way, and strictly between you and me, I have a shrewd suspicion that Uriah Heep wasn't the only cad in David Copperfield.

Brutus, the originator of the saying, took the tide at the flood, and it led him and his friends on to death, or—well, perhaps, under the circumstances, it was all the same to Brutus and his old mate, Cassius.

And this, my masters, brings me home, Bush-born bard, to Ancient Rome.

And there's little difference in the climate, or the men—save in the little matter of ironmongery—and no difference at all in the women.

We'll pass over the accident that happened to Caesar. Such accidents had happened to great and little Caesars hundreds of times before, and have happened many times since, and will happen until the end of time, both in "sport" (in plays) and in earnest:

CASSIUS
....How many ages hence Shall this our lofty scene be acted over In states unborn and accents yet unknown?

BRUTUS
How many times shall Caesar bleed in sport, That now at Pompey's basis lies along No worthier than the dust!

Shakespeare hadn't Australia and George Rignold in his mind's eye when he wrote that.

CASSIUS
So oft as that shall be, So often shall the knot of us be call'd The men that gave their country liberty.

Well, be that as it will, I'm with Brutus too, irrespective of the merits of the case. Antony spoke at the funeral, with free and generous permission, and see what he made of it. And why shouldn't I? and see what I'll make of it.

Antony, after sending abject and uncalled-for surrender, and grovelling unasked in the dust to Brutus and his friends as no straight mate should do for another, dead or alive—and after taking the blood-stained hands of his alleged friend's murderers—got permission to speak. To speak for his own ends or that paltry, selfish thing called "revenge," be it for one's self or one's friend.

"Brutus, I want a word with you," whispered Cassius. "Don't let him speak! You don't know how he might stir up the mob with what he says."

But Brutus had already given his word:

ANTONY
That's all I seek: And am moreover suitor that I may Produce his body to the market place, And in the pulpit, as becomes a friend, Speak in the order of his funeral.

BRUTUS
You shall, Mark Antony.

And now, strong in his right, as he thinks, and trusting to the honour of Antony, he only stipulates that he (Brutus) shall go on to the platform first and explain things; and that Antony shall speak all the good he can of Caesar, but not abuse Brutus and his friends.

And Antony (mark you) agrees and promises and breaks his promise immediately afterwards. Maybe he was only gaining time for his good friend Octavius Caesar, but time gained by such foul means is time lost through all eternity. Did Mark think of these things years afterwards in Egypt when he was doubly ruined and doubly betrayed to his good friend Octavius by that hot, jealous, selfish, shallow, shifty, strumpet, Cleopatra, and Octavius was after his scalp with a certainty of getting it? He did—and he spoke of it, too.

Brutus made his speech, a straightforward, manly speech in prose, and the gist of the matter was that he did what he did (killed Caesar), not because he loved Caesar less, but because he loved Rome more. And I believe he told the simple honest truth.

Then he acts as Antony's chairman, or introducer, in a manly straightforward manner, and then he goes off and leaves the stage to him, which is another generous act; though it was lucky for Brutus, as it happened afterwards, that he was out of the way.

Mark Antony gets all the limelight and blank verse. He had the "gift of the gab" all right. Old Cassius referred to it later on in one of those "words-before-blows" barneys they had on the battlefield where they hurt each other a damned sight more with their tongues than they did with their swords afterwards.

We've all heard of Antony's speech:

I come to bury Caesar, not to praise him.

Which was a lie to start with.

The evil that men do lives after them, The good is oft interred with their bones.

Which is not so true in these days of newspapers and magazines. And so on. He says that Brutus and his friends are honourable men about nine times in his short speech. Now, was Mark Antony an honourable man?

And then the flap-doodle about dead Caesar's wounds, and their poor dumb mouths, and the people kissing them, and dipping their handkerchiefs in his sacred blood. All worthy of our Purves trying to pump tears out of a jury.

But it fetched the crowd; it always did, it always has done, it always does, and it always will do. And the hint of Caesar's will, and the open abuse of Brutus and Co. when he saw that he was safe, and the cheap anti-climax of the reading of the will. Nothing in this line can be too cheap for the crowd, as witness the melodramas of our own civilized and enlightened times.

Antony was a noble Purves.

And the mob rushed off to burn houses, as it has always done, and will always do when it gets a chance—it tried to burn mine more than once.

The quarrel scene between Brutus and Cassius is one of the best scenes in Shakespeare. It is great from the sublime to the ridiculous—you must read it for yourself. It seems that Brutus objected to Cassius's, or one of his off-side friends' methods of raising the wind—he reckoned it was one of the very things they killed Julius Caesar for; and Cassius, loving Brutus more than a brother, is very much hurt about it. I can't make out what the trouble really was about and I don't suppose either Cassius or Brutus was clear as to what it was all about either. It's generally the way when friends fall out. It seems also that Brutus thinks that Cassius refused to lend him a few quid to pay his legions, and, you know, it's an unpardonable crime for one mate to refuse another a few quid when he's in a hole; but it seems that the messenger was but a fool who brought Cassius's answer back. It is generally the messenger who is to blame, when friends make it up after a quarrel that was all their own fault. Messengers had an uncomfortable time in those days, as witness the case of the base slave who had to bring Cleopatra the news of Antony's marriage with Octavia.

But the quarrel scene is great for its deep knowledge of the hearts of men in matters of man to man—of man friend to man friend—and it is as humanly simple as a barney between two old bush mates that threatens to end in a bloody fist-fight and separation for life, but chances to end in a beer. This quarrel threatened to end in the death of either Brutus or Cassius or a set-to between their two armies, just at the moment when they all should have been knit together against the forces of Mark Antony and Octavius Caesar; but it ended in a beer, or its equivalent, a bowl of wine.

Earlier in the quarrel, where Brutus asks why, after striking down the foremost man in all the world for supporting land agents and others, should they do the same thing and contaminate their fingers with base bribes?

I'd rather be a dog and bay the moon, Than such a Roman.

CASSIUS says:
Brutus, bait not me I'll not endure it: you forget yourself,
To hedge me in; I am a soldier, I,
Older in practice, abler than yourself
To make conditions.

BRUTUS
Go to, you are not, Cassius.

CASSIUS
I am.

BRUTUS
I say you are not.
And so they get to it again until:

CASSIUS

Is it come to this?

BRUTUS

You say you are a better soldier:
Let it appear so; make your vaunting true,
And it shall please me well: for mine own part,
I shall be glad to learn of noble men.

CASSIUS

You wrong me every way; you wrong me,
Brutus; I said, an elder soldier, not a better.
Did I say better?

(What big boys they were—and what big boys we all are!)

BRUTUS

If you did, I care not.

CASSIUS

When Caesar lived he durst not thus have moved me.

BRUTUS

Peace, peace! you durst not thus have tempted him.

CASSIUS

I durst not!

BRUTUS

No.

CASSIUS

What! Durst not tempt him!

BRUTUS

For your life you durst not.

CASSIUS

Do not presume too much upon my love;
I may do that I shall be sorry for.

BRUTUS

You have done that you should be sorry for.

And so on till he gets to the matter of the refused quids, which is cleared up at the expense of the messenger.

CASSIUS

.... Brutus hath rived my heart
A friend should bear his friend's infirmities,
But Brutus makes mine greater than they are.

BRUTUS
I do not, till you practise them on me.

CASSIUS
You love me not.

BRUTUS
I do not like your faults.

CASSIUS
A friendly eye could never see such faults.

BRUTUS
A flatterer's would not, though they do appear
As huge as high Olympus.

Then Cassius lets himself go. He calls on Antony and young Octavius and all the rest of 'em to come and be revenged on him alone, for he's tired of the world ("Cassius is aweary of the world," he says). He's hated by one he loves (that's Brutus). He's braved by his "brother" (Brutus), checked like a bondman, and Brutus keeps an eye on all his faults and puts 'em down in a note-book, and learns 'em over and gets 'em off by memory to cast in his teeth. He offers Brutus his dagger and bare breast and wants Brutus to take out his heart, which, he says, is richer than all the quids—or rather gold—which Brutus said he wouldn't lend him. He wants Brutus to strike him as he did Caesar, for he reckons that when Brutus hated Caesar worst he loved him far better than ever he loved Cassius.

Remember these men were Southerners, like ourselves, not cold-blooded Northerners—and, in spite of the seemingly effeminate Italian temperament, as brave as our men were at Elands River. The reason of Brutus's seeming coldness and hardness during the quarrel is set forth in a startling manner later on, as only the greatest poet in this world could do it.

Brutus tells him kindly to put up his pig-sticker (and button his shirt) and he could be just as mad or good-tempered as he liked, and do what he liked, Brutus wouldn't mind him:

.... Dishonour shall be humour.
O Cassius, you are yoked with a lamb
That carries anger as the flint bears fire,
Who, much enforced, shows a hasty spark
And straight is cold again.

Whereupon Cassius weeps because he thinks Brutus is laughing at him.

Hath Cassius lived
To be but mirth and laughter to his Brutus,
When grief and blood ill-temper'd vexeth him.

BRUTUS
When I spoke that, I was ill-temper'd too.

CASSIUS
Do you confess so much? Give me your hand.

BRUTUS
And my heart too.

Then Cassius explains that he got his temper from his mother (as I did mine).

CASSIUS
O Brutus!

BRUTUS
What's the matter? [Shakespeare should have added `now.']

CASSIUS
Have not you love enough to bear with me,
When that rash humour which my mother gave me
Makes me forgetful?

BRUTUS
Yes, Cassius, and from henceforth,
When you are over-earnest with your Brutus,
He'll think your mother chides, and leave you so.

And all this on the brink of disaster and death.

But here comes a rare touch, and we might as well quote it in full.

Mind you, I am following Shakespeare, and not history, which is mostly lies.

A great poet's instinct might be nearer the truth; after all. Of course scholars know that Macbeth (or Macbethad) reigned for upwards of twenty years in Scotland a wise and a generous king—so much so that he was called "Macbathad the Liberal," and it was Duncan who found his way to the throne by way of murder; but it didn't fit in with Shakespeare's plans, and—anyway that's only a little matter between the ghosts of Bill and Mac which was doubtless fixed up long ago. More likely they thought it such a one-millionth part of a trifle that they never dreamed of thinking of mentioning it.

(Noise within.)

POET (within):
Let me go in to see the generals;
There is some grudge between 'em—'tis not meet
They be alone.

LUCILIUS (within):
You shall not come to them.

POET (within):
Nothing but death shall stay me.

("Within" in this case is, of course, without—outside the tent where Lucilius and Titinius are on guard.)

Enter **POET**.

CASSIUS
How now! What's the matter?

POET
For shame, you generals! What do you mean?
Love, and be friends, as two such men should be:
For I have seen more years, I'm sure, than ye.

CASSIUS
Ha, ha! how vilely doth this cynic rhyme!

BRUTUS
Get you hence, sirrah; saucy fellow, hence!

CASSIUS
Bear with him, Brutus; 'tis his fashion.

BRUTUS
I'll know his humour when he knows his time:
What should the wars do with these jingling fools?
Companion, hence!

CASSIUS
Away, away, be gone!

(Exit **POET**.)

Blessed are the peacemakers, for they shall inherit a black eye (Lawson). Shakespeare was ever rough on poets—but stay! Consider that this great world of Rome and all the men and women in it were created by a "jingling fool" and a master of bad—not to say execrable—rhymes, and his name was William Shakespeare. You need to sit down and think awhile after that.

Brutus sends Lucilius and Titinius to bid the commanders lodge their companies for the night, and then all come to him. Then he gives Cassius a shock and strikes him to the heart for his share in the quarrel. It is almost directly after the row, when they have kicked out the "jingling fool" of a poet. Cassius does not know that Brutus has to-day received news of the death, in Rome, of his good and true wife Portia, who, during a fit of insanity, brought on by her grief and anxiety for Brutus, and in the absence of her attendant, has poisoned herself—or "swallowed fire," as Shakespeare has it.

BRUTUS (to Lucius, his servant):
Lucius, a bowl of wine!

CASSIUS
I did not think you could have been so angry.

BRUTUS
O Cassius, I am sick of many griefs.

CASSIUS
Of your philosophy you make no use,
If you give place to accidental evils.

BRUTUS
No man bears sorrow better:—Portia is dead.

CASSIUS
Ha! Portia!

BRUTUS
She is dead.

CASSIUS
How 'scaped I killing when I cross'd you so!
O insupportable and touching loss!
Upon what sickness?

BRUTUS
Impatient of my absence,
And grief that young Octavius with Mark Antony
Have made themselves so strong: for with her death
That tidings came; with this she fell distract,
And, her attendants absent, swallowed fire.

CASSIUS
And died so?

BRUTUS
Even so.

CASSIUS
O, ye immortal gods!

(Enter Lucius, with a jar of wine, a goblet, and a taper.)

BRUTUS
Speak no more of her. Give me a bowl of wine:

In this I bury all unkindness, Cassius.

(Drinks.)

CASSIUS
My heart is thirsty for that noble pledge.
Fill, Lucius, till the wine o'erswell the cup;
I cannot drink too much of Brutus' love.

(Drinks.)

You ought to read that scene carefully. It will do no one any harm. It did me a lot of good one time, when I was about to quarrel with a friend whose heart was sick with many griefs that I knew nothing of at the time. You never know what's behind.

Titinius and Messala come in, and proceed to discuss the situation.

BRUTUS
Come in, Titinius!! Welcome, good Messala.
Now sit we close about this taper here,
And call in question our necessities.

CASSIUS (on whom the wine seems to have taken some effect)
Portia, art thou gone?

BRUTUS
No more, I pray you. Messala, I have here received letters,
That young Octavius and Mark Antony
Come down upon us with a mighty power,
Bending their expedition towards Philippi.

Messala has also letters to the same purpose, and they have likewise news of the murder, or execution, of upwards of a hundred senators in Rome.

CASSIUS
Cicero one!

MESSALA
Cicero is dead.

Poor Brutus! His heart had cause to be sick of many griefs that day. Messala thinks he has news to break, and Brutus draws him out. How many and many a man and woman, with a lump in the throat, have broken sad and bad news since that day, and started out to do it in the same old gentle way:

MESSALA
Had you your letters from your wife, my lord?

BRUTUS

No, Messala.

MESSALA
Nor nothing in your letters writ of her?

BRUTUS
Nothing, Messala.

MESSALA
That, methinks, is strange.

BRUTUS
Why ask you? Hear you aught of her in yours?

Maybe it strikes Messala like a flash that Brutus is in no need of any more bad news just now, and it had better be postponed till after the battle:

MESSALA
No, my lord.

BRUTUS
Now, as you are a Roman, tell me true.

MESSALA
Then like a Roman bear the truth I tell:
For certain she is dead, and by strange manner.

BRUTUS
Why, farewell, Portia. We must die,

MESSALA
With meditating that she must die once
I have the patience to endure it now.

Poor Messala comes to the scratch again rather lamely with a little weak flattery: "Even so great men great losses should endure;" and Cassius says, rather mixedly—it might have been the wine—that he has as much strength in bearing trouble as Brutus has, and yet he couldn't bear it so.

I have as much of this in art as you,
But yet my nature could not bear it so.

BRUTUS
Well, to our work alive. What do you think
Of marching on Philippi presently?

Brutus was a strong man. Portia's spirit must bide a while. They discuss a plan of campaign. Cassius is for waiting for the enemy to seek them and so get through his tucker and knock his men up, while they rest in a good position; but Brutus argues that the enemy will gather up the country people between Philippi and their camp and come on refreshed with added numbers and courage, and it would be better for them to meet him at Philippi with these people at their back. The politics or inclination of the said country people didn't matter in those days. "There is a tide in the affairs of men"—and so they decide to take it at the flood and float high on to the rocks at Philippi. Ah well, it led on to immortality, if it didn't to fortune.

Well, there's no more to say. Brutus thinks that the main thing now is a little rest—in which you'll agree with him; and he sends for his night-shirt.

Good night, Titinius: noble, noble Cassius,
Good night, and good repose!

That old fool of a Cassius—remorseful old smooth-bore—is still a bit maudlin—maybe he had another swig at the wine when Shakespeare wasn't looking.

CASSIUS
O my dear brother! This was an ill beginning of the night
Never come such division 'tween our souls!
Let it not, Brutus.

BRUTUS
Everything is well.

CASSIUS
Good night, my lord.

BRUTUS
Good sight, good brother.

TITINIUS and **MESSALA**
Good night, Lord Brutus.

BRUTUS
Farewell, every one.

And Cassius is the man whom Caesar denounced as having a lean and hungry look: "Let me have men about me that are fat... such men are dangerous." (Mr Archibald held with that—and he had a lean, if not a hungry, look too.) When Antony put in a word for Cassius, Caesar said that he wished he was fatter anyhow. "He thinks too much," Caesar said to Antony. He read a lot; he could look through men; he never went to the theatre, and heard no music; he never smiled except as if grinning sarcastically at himself for "being moved to smile at anything." Caesar said that such men were never at heart's ease while they could see a bigger man than themselves, and therefore such men were dangerous. "Come on my right hand, for this ear is deaf, and tell me truly what thou think'st of him." (That's a touch, for deafness in people affected that way is usually greater in the left ear.)

When Lucilius returned from taking a message from Brutus to Cassius re the loan of the fivers aforementioned and other matters—and before the arrival of Cassius with his horse and foot, and the quarrel—Brutus asked Lucilius what sort of a reception he had, and being told "With courtesy and respect enough," he remarked, "Thou hast described a hot friend cooling," and so on. But Cassius will cool no more until death cools him to-morrow at Philippi.

The rare gentleness of Brutus's character—and of the characters of thousands of other bosses in trouble—is splendidly, and ah! so softly, pictured in the tent with his servants after the departure of the others. It is a purely domestic scene without a hint of home, women, or children—save that they themselves are big children. The scene now has the atmosphere of a soft, sad nightfall, after a long, long, hot and weary day full of toil and struggle and trouble—though it is really well on towards morning.

Lucius comes in with the gown. Brutus says, "Give me the gown," and asks where his (Lucius's) musical instrument is, and Lucius replies that it's here in the tent. Brutus notices that he speaks drowsily. "Poor knave, I blame thee not, thou are o'er-watched." He tells him to call Claudius and some other of his men: "I'd have them sleep on cushions in my tent." They come. He tells them he might have to send them on business by and by to his "brother" Cassius, and bids them lie down and sleep, calling them sirs. They say they'll stand and watch his pleasure. "I will not have it so; lie down, good sirs." He finds, in the pocket of his gown, a book he'd been hunting high and low for—and had evidently given Lucius a warm time about—and he draws Lucius's attention to the fact:

Look, Lucius, here's the book I sought for so:
I put it in the pocket of my gown.

LUCIUS
I was sure your lordship did not give it to me.

BRUTUS
Bear with me, good boy, I am much forgetful, etc.

He asks Lucius if he can hold up his heavy eyes and touch his instrument a strain or two. But better give it all—it's not long:

LUCIUS
Ay, my lord, an't please you.

BRUTUS
It does, my boy: I trouble thee too much, but thou art willing.

LUCIUS
It is my duty, sir.

BRUTUS
I should not urge thy duty past thy might;
I know young bloods look for a time of rest.

LUCIUS
I have slept, my lord, already.

BRUTUS

It was well done; and thou shalt sleep again; I will not hold thee long: if I do live, I will be good to thee. (Music, and a song.) This is a sleepy tune. O murderous slumber, Lay'st thou thy leaden mace upon my boy That plays thee music? Gentle knave, good-night; I will not do thee so much wrong to wake thee: If thou dost nod, thou break'st thy instrument; I'll take it from thee; and, good boy, good-night. Let me see, let me see; is not the leaf turn'd down Where I left reading? Here it is, I think.

(He sits down.)

A man for all time! How natural it all reads! You must remember that he is a tired man after a long, strenuous day such as none of us ever know. The fate of Rome and his—a much smaller matter—are hanging on the balance, and tomorrow will decide; but he is so mind-dulled and shoulder-weary under the tremendous burden of great things and of many griefs that he is almost apathetic; and over all is the cloud of a loss that he has not yet had time to realize. He is self-hypnotized, so to speak, and his mind mercifully dulled for the moment on the Sea of Fatalism.

(Enter **GHOST of CAESAR**

BRUTUS
How ill this taper burns! Ha! who comes here?
I think it is the weakness of mine eyes
That shapes this monstrous apparition. It comes upon me.
Art thou any thing? Art thou some god, some angel, or some devil
That makest my blood cold, and my hair to stare?
Speak to me what thou art!

His very "scare," or rather his cold blood and staring hair are as things apart, to be analysed and explained quickly and put aside.

GHOST
Thy evil spirit, Brutus.

That was frank enough, anyway.

BRUTUS
Why comest thou?

GHOST
To tell thee thou shalt see me at Philippi.

BRUTUS
Well; then I shall see thee again?

GHOST
Ay, at Philippi.

(Vanishes.)

That was very satisfactory, so far. But Brutus, having taken heart, as he says, would hold more talk with the "ill spirit." A ghost always needs to be taken quietly—it's no use getting excited and threshing round. But Caesar's, being a new-chum ghost and bashful, was doubtless embarrassed by his cool, matter-of-fact reception, and left. It didn't matter much. They were to meet soon, above Philippi, on more level terms.

But I cannot get away from the idea that Caesar's ghost's visit was made in a friendly spirit. Who knows? Perhaps Portia's spirit had sent it to comfort Brutus: her own being prevented from going for some reason only known to the immortal gods.

Then Brutus wakes them all.

LUCIUS
The strings, my lord, are false.

BRUTUS
He thinks he is still at his instrument. Lucius, awake!

And after questioning them as to whether they cried out in their sleep, or saw anything, he bids the boy sleep again (it is easy for tired boys to sleep at will in camp) and sends two of the others to Cassius to bid him get his forces on the way early and he would follow.

BRUTUS
Go and commend me to my brother Cassius;
Bid him set on his powers betimes before,
And we will follow.

VARRO and **CLAUDIUS**
It shall be done, my lord.

For, being a wise soldier, as well as a brave and gentle one, he reckoned, no doubt, that it would be best to have a strong man in the rear until the field was actually reached, for the benefit of would-be deserters, and unconsidered trifles of country people-and maybe for another reason not totally disconnected with his erratic friend Cassius.

Just one more scene, and a very different one, before we hurry on to the end, as they have done to Philippi. It's the only scene in which those two unlucky Romans, Cassius and Brutus, seem to score.

It is during the barney, or as Shakespeare calls it, the "parley" before the battle. Those parleys never seemed to do any good—except to make matters worse, if I might put it like that: it's the same, under similar circumstances, right up to to-day. Enter on one side Octavius Caesar, Mark Antony, and their pals and army; and, on the other, Brutus and Cassius and the friends and followers of their falling fortunes.

BRUTUS
Words before blows: is it so, countrymen?

OCTAVIUS
Not that we love words better, as you do.

You see, Octavius starts it.

Brutus lays himself open:

BRUTUS
Good words are better than bad strokes, Octavius.

ANTONY
In your bad strokes, Brutus, you give good words:
Witness the hole you made in Caesar's heart,
Crying, "Long live! hail, Caesar!"

This is one for Brutus, though it contains a lie. But Cassius comes to the rescue:

CASSIUS
Antony,
The posture of your blows are yet unknown,
But, for your words, they rob the Hybla bees
And leave them honeyless.

ANTONY
Not stingless too.

BRUTUS
O, yes, and soundless too;
For you have stol'n their buzzing, Antony,
And very wisely threat before you sting.

That was one for Antony, and he gets mad. "Villains!" he yells, and he abuses them about their vile daggers hacking one another in the sides of Caesar (a little matter that ought to be worn threadbare by now), and calls them apes and hounds and bondmen and curs, and O, flatterers (which seems to be worst of all in his opinion—for he isn't one, you know), and damns 'em generally.

Old Cassius remarks, "Flatterers!"

Then Octavius breaks loose, and draws his Roman chopper and waves it round, and spreads himself out over Caesar's three-and-thirty wounds—which ought to be given a rest by this time, but only seem to be growing in number—and swears that he won't put up said chopper till said wounds are avenged,

Or till another Caesar
Have added slaughter to the sword of traitors.

Brutus says quietly that he cannot die by traitors unless he brings 'em with him. (He sent one to Egypt later on.) Octavius says he hopes he wasn't born to die on Brutus's sword; and Brutus says, in effect, that even if he was any good he couldn't die more honourably.

BRUTUS

O, if thou wert the noblest of thy strain,
Young man, thou couldst not die more honourable.

CASSIUS
A peevish schoolboy, worthless of such honour,
Join'd with a masker and a reveller!

Octavius calls off his dogs, and tells them to come on to-day if they dare, or if not, when they have stomachs.

CASSIUS
Why, now, blow wind, swell billow, and swim bark!
The storm is up, and all is on the hazard.

Yes, I reckon old Cassius ("old" in an affectionate sense) and Brutus came out top dogs from that scrap anyway. And, yes, Antony was good at orating. He was great at orating over dead men—especially dead "friends" (as he called his rivals) and dead enemies. Brutus was "the noblest Roman of them all" when Antony came across him stiff later on. Now when I die—

Octavius, by the way, orated over Antony and his dusky hussy later on in Egypt, and they were the most "famous pair" in the world. I wonder whether the grim humour of it struck Octavius then: but then that young man seemed to have but little brains and less humour.

But now they go to see about settling the matter with ironmongery. You can imagine the fight; the heat and the dust, for it was spring in a climate like ours. The bullocking, sweating, grunting, slaughter, the crack and clash and rattle as of fire-irons in a fender. The bad Latin language; the running away and chasing en masse and by individuals. The mutual pauses, the truces or spells—"smoke-ho's" we'd call 'em—between masses and individuals. The battered-in, lost, discarded or stolen helmets; the blood-stained, dinted, and loosened armour with bits missing, and the bloody and grotesque bandages. The confusion amongst the soldiers, as it is to-day—the ignorance of one wing as to the fate of the other, of one party as to the fate of the other, of one individual as to the fate of another:

BRUTUS
Ride, ride, Messala, ride, and give these bills [directions to officers]
Unto the legions on the other side:

Poor Cassius, routed and in danger of being surrounded, and thinking Brutus is in the same plight, or a prisoner or dead—and that Titinius is taken or killed—gets his bondman, whose life he once saved, to kill him in return for his freedom.

Stand not to answer: here, take thou the hilts;
And when my face is cover 'd, as 'tis now,
Guide thou the sword.
Caesar, thou art revenged,
Even with the sword that kill'd thee.

Good-bye, Cassius, old chap!

Titinius and Messala, coming too late, find Cassius dead; and Titinius, being left alone while Messala takes the news to Brutus, kills himself with Cassius's sword. Titinius, farewell!

Come Brutus and those that are left.

BRUTUS
Where, where, Messala, doth his body lie?

MESSALA
Lo, yonder, and Titinius mourning it.

BRUTUS
Titinius' face is upward.

CATO
He is slain.

Grim mates in a grim day in a grim hour. Then the cry of Brutus:

O Julius Caesar, thou art mighty yet!

But if he were, perhaps he only gathered old Cassius and Titinius to be sure of their company with him and Brutus amongst the gods a little later.

BRUTUS
Friends, I owe more tears
To this dead man than you shall see me pay.
I shall find time, Cassius, I shall find time.

And, after making arrangements for the removal of Cassius's body, they go to try their fortunes in a second fight. Young Cato is killed and good Lucilius taken. Comes Brutus beaten, with Dardanius his last friend, and his three servants, Clitus, Strato, and Volumnius.

BRUTUS
Come, poor remains of friends, rest on this rock.

Strato, exhausted, goes to sleep, as man can sleep during a battle; and Brutus whispers the others, one after another, to kill him; but they are shocked and refuse: "I'll rather kill myself," "I do such a deed?" etc. He begs Volumnius, his old schoolmate, to hold his sword-hilt while he runs on it, for their love of old.

VOLUMNIUS
That's not the office for a friend, my lord.
There are alarums, and they urge him to fly, for it's no use stopping there.

BRUTUS
Farewell to you; and you; and you, Volumnius.
Strato, thou hast been all this while asleep;

Farewell to thee too, Strato! Countrymen,
My heart doth joy that yet in all my life
I found so man but he was true to me.

Ye gods! but it's grand. I wish to our God that I could say as much—or that man or woman [n]ever found me untrue. Could Antony say as much, afterwards, in Egypt—or Octavius! with Antony then on his mind? Even Antony's last man and servant failed him in the end, killing himself rather than kill his master. But Strato—

There are more alarums and voices calling to them to run. They urge Brutus again, and he tells them to go and he'll follow. They all run except Strato, who hesitates.

BRUTUS
I prithee, Strato, stay thou by thy lord:
Thou art a fellow of a good respect;
Thy life hath had some snatch of honour in it
Hold then my sword, and turn away thy face,
While I do run upon it. Wilt thou, Strato?

STRATO
Give me your hand first: fare you well, my lord.

BRUTUS
Farewell, good Strato. Caesar, now be still:
I kill'd not thee with half so good a will.

Brutus, good night!

I like Shakespeare's servants. They seem to show that he sprang from servants or common people rather than from lords and masters, for he deals with them very gently. It must be understood that servants, bond and free, were born unto the same house and served it for generations; and so down to modern England, where the old nurse and the tottering old gardener often nursed and played with "Master Will," when his father, the dead and gone old squire, was a young man.

See where Timon's servants stand in the only patch of sunlight in that black and bitter story:

Enter Flavius, with two or three **SERVANTS**.

FIRST SERVANT
Hear you, master steward, where's our master?
Are we undone? cast off? nothing remaining?

FLAVIUS
Alack, my fellows, what should I say to you?
Let me be recorded by the righteous gods,
I am as poor as you.

FIRST SERVANT

Such a house broke!
So noble a master fall'n! All gone! and not
One friend to take his fortune by the arm,
And go along with him!

SECOND SERVANT
As we do turn our backs
From our companion thrown into his grave,
So his familiars to his buried fortunes
Slink all away; leave their false vows with him,
Like empty purses pick'd; and his poor self,
A dedicated beggar to the air,
With his disease of all-shunn'd poverty,
Walks, like contempt, alone. More of our fellows.

Enter other **SERVANTS**.

FLAVIUS
All broken implements of a ruin'd house.

THIRD SERVANT
Yet do our hearts wear Timon's livery;
That see I by our faces; we are fellows still,
Serving alike in sorrow: leak'd is our bark,
And we, poor mates, stand on the dying deck,
Hearing the surges threat; we must all part
Into this sea of air.

FLAVIUS
Good fellows all,
The latest of my wealth I'll share amongst you.
Wherever we shall meet, for Timon's sake
Let's yet be fellows; let's shake our heads, and say,
As 'twere a knell unto our master's fortunes,
"We have seen better days." Let each take some.

(Giving them money.)

Nay, put out all your hands. Not one word more:
Thus part we rich in sorrow, parting poor.

Notes on Australianisms. Based on my own speech over the years, with some checking in the dictionaries. Not all of these are peculiar to Australian slang, but are important in Lawson's stories, and carry overtones.

barrackers: people who cheer for a sporting team, etc. boko: crazy. bushman/bushwoman: someone who lives an isolated existence, far from cities, "in the bush", "outback". (today: "bushy". In New Zealand it is a timber getter. Lawson was sacked from a forestry job in New Zealand, "because he wasn't a *bushman":) bushranger: an Australian ``highwayman'', who lived in the `bush'— scrub—and attacked and robbed, especially gold carrying coaches and banks. Romanticised as anti-authoritarian Robin Hood figures— cf. Ned Kelly—but usually very violent. US use was very different (more = explorer), though some lexicographers think the word (along with "bush" in this sense) was borrowed from the US... churchyarder: Sounding as if dying—ready for the churchyard = cemetery cobber: mate, friend. Used to be derived from Hebrew chaver via Yiddish. General opinion now seems to be that it entered the language too early for that—and an English etymology is preferred. fiver: a five pound (sterling) note (or "bill") fossick: pick out gold, in a fairly desultory fashion. In old "mullock" heaps or crvices in rocks. jackaroo: (Jack + kangaroo; sometimes jackeroo)—someone, in early days a new immigrant from England, learning to work on a sheep/cattle station (U.S. "ranch".) kiddy: young child. "kid" plus ubiquitous Australia "-y" or "-ie" nobbler: a drink, esp. of spirits overlanding: driving (or, "droving", cattle from pasture to market or railhead.) pannikin: a metal mug. Pipeclay: or Eurunderee, Where Lawson spent much of his early life (including his three years of school... Poley: name for s hornless (or dehorned) cow. skillion(-room): A "lean-to", a room built up against the back of some other building, with separate roof. sliprails: portion of a fence where the rails are lossely fitted so that they may be removed from one side and animal let through. smoke-ho: a short break from, esp., heavy physical work, and those who wish to can smoke. sov.: sovereign, gold coin worth one pound sterling splosh: money Sqinny: nickname for someone with a squint. Stousher: nickname for someone often in a fight (or "stoush") swagman (swaggy): Generally, anyone who is walking in the "outback" with a swag. (See "The Romance of the Swag".) Lawson also restricts it at times to those whom he considers to be tramps, not looking for work but for "handouts" (i.e., "bums" in US. In view of the Great Depression, 1890, perhaps unfairly. In 1892 it was reckoned 1/3 men were out of work)*

GJC

Henry Lawson – A Short Biography

Henry Archibald Hertzberg Lawson was born on the 17th June 1867 in a town on the Grenfell goldfields of New South Wales, Australia.

His parents, father Niel, a Norwegian born miner and mother Louisa, a noted poet, publisher and feminist were married on 7th July 1866 when he was 32 and she 18. On Henry's birth, the family surname was Anglicised to Lawson. The couple were to have an unhappy marriage despite producing three children.

Lawson attended school at Eurunderee from October 1876 but an ear infection he contracted left him partially deaf. By fourteen he had lost his hearing completely.

Lawson later attended a Catholic school at Mudgee, New South Wales where he developed an interest in poetry and, on his mother's influence, immersed himself in books given that learning in the classroom, with his deafness, was a major hurdle.

In 1883, after working on construction jobs with his father in the Blue Mountains, Lawson joined his mother in Sydney where she was living with his siblings. Here, Lawson worked during the day and studied at night for his matriculation in the hopes of enrolling at university. However, he failed his exams.

His first published poem was 'A Song of the Republic' in The Bulletin on 1st October 1887. This was quickly followed by other published poems with one recognising him as "a youth whose poetic genius here speaks eloquently for itself."

In 1890 he began a relationship with Mary Gilmore but it broke down due to his frequent absences from Sydney.

Lawson received an offer to write for the Brisbane Boomerang in 1891, but financial troubles at the magazine made this a short stint of only a few months. Despite writing for other magazines in Brisbane it was a dead end.

He returned to Sydney and continued to write for the Bulletin which, in 1892, engaged him for an inland trip where he could write articles about the harsh realities of life in drought-stricken New South Wales. He also took some time to work as a roustabout (an unskilled or semi-skilled worker) in the woolshed at Toorale Station. This resulted in his contributions to the Bulletin Debate and became the experience he used for a number of his stories in subsequent years. For Lawson this was an eye-opening period. His grim view of the outback was far removed from the romantic idyll of bravery and beauty inked in the poetry of his contemporary Banjo Paterson.

In 1896, Lawson married Bertha Bredt, Jr., daughter of Bertha Bredt, the prominent socialist. The marriage ended very unhappily in June 1903. They had two children.

Despite this Lawson was finding his way in the literary world. His writing was achieving recognition. His most successful prose collection 'While the Billy Boils', was published in 1896. In it he virtually reinvented Australian realism.

His writing style of short, sharp sentences with honed and sparse descriptions created a personal writing style that defined Australians: dryly laconic, passionately egalitarian and deeply humane. Most of Lawson's work centres on the Australian bush, it's fabled outback, such as in the desolate 'Past Carin', and is considered by many to vividly portray the real Australian life at that time.

Like the majority of Australians, Lawson lived in a city, but had had plenty of experience in outback life, these two outlooks helped shape a very individual talent. Unfortunately, his life was also flawed with other issues.

In Sydney in 1898 he was a prominent member of the Dawn and Dusk Club, a bohemian club of writer friends who met for drinks and conversation.

Sadly, for Lawson despite his growing recognition and fame he became withdrawn and unable to take part in the usual routines of life. His struggles with alcohol and mental health issues continued to drain him. His once prolific literary output began to decline. At times he was destitute mainly due, despite good sales and an enthusiastic audience, to ruinous publishing deals he had entered into.

In 1903 he bought a room at Mrs Isabel Byers' Coffee Palace in North Sydney. This near 20-year friendship between Mrs Byers and Lawson was a bedrock for him. Despite his position as the most celebrated Australian writer of the time, Lawson was deeply depressed and perpetually poor. His ex-wife repeatedly reported him for non-payment of child maintenance, which resulted in numerous jail terms or periods in psychiatric institutions. He was incarcerated at Darlinghurst Gaol for drunkenness, wife desertion, child desertion, and non-payment of child support seven times between 1905 and 1909 and spent a total of 159 days in prison. He wrote about these experiences in the haunting poem 'One Hundred and Three'—his prison number—which was published in 1908.

Mrs Byers was a good poet herself and, although of modest education, had been writing vivid poetry since her teens in a somewhat similar style to Lawson's. Long separated from her husband and elderly, Mrs Byers was, at the time she met Lawson, a woman of independent means looking forward to a comfortable retirement. She regarded Lawson as Australia's greatest living poet, and hoped to sustain him well enough to keep him writing. She acted as his agent in negotiations with publishers, helped to arrange contact with his children, contacted friends and supporters to help him financially, as well as assisting and nursing him through his mental health issues and problems with alcohol. She wrote countless letters on his behalf and pursued any avenue that could provide Lawson with financial support or a publishing deal.

Regardless of all else Lawson was a vocal nationalist and republican and took pride that many of his works were helping to establish the Australian vernacular in fiction.

Henry Archibald Hertzberg Lawson died, of a cerebral hemorrhage, in Mrs Byer's home in Abbotsford, Sydney on 2nd September 1922.

Lawson became the first Australian writer to be granted a state funeral. It was attended by the Prime Minister Billy Hughes and the (later) Premier of New South Wales, Jack Lang (the husband of Lawson's sister-in-law Hilda Bredt), as well as thousands of citizens.

Henry Lawson – A Concise Bibliography

Short Stories in Prose and Verse (1894)
While the Billy Boils (1896)
In the Days When the World was Wide and Other Verses (1896)
Verses, Popular and Humorous (1900)
On the Track (1900)
Over the Sliprails (1900)
On the Track, and, Over the Sliprails (1900)
Popular Verses (1900)
Humorous Verses (1900)
The Country I Come From (1901)
Joe Wilson and His Mates (1901)
Children of the Bush (1902)
When I Was King and Other Verses (1905)
The Elder Son (1905)
When I Was King (1905)
The Romance of the Swag (1907)
Send Round the Hat (1907)
The Skyline Riders and Other Verses (1910)
The Rising of the Court and Other Sketches in Prose and Verse (1910)

For Australia and Other Poems (1913)
Triangles of Life and Other Stories (1913)
My Army, O, My Army! and Other Songs (1915)
Song of the Dardanelles and Other Verses (1916)
Selected Poems of Henry Lawson (1918)

www.ingramcontent.com/pod-product-compliance
Lightning Source LLC
Chambersburg PA
CBHW021938170626
46807CB00007B/3180